The Butterfly *Inside*

One women's experiences through the challenges of having trans family members while being a sister, daughter, mother.

Written by Jessica L Rose

The Butterfly *Inside*

"No one is born hating another person because of the colour of his skin, or his background, or his religion. People must learn to hate, and if they can learn to hate, they can be taught to love, for love comes more naturally to the human heart than its opposite." Nelson Mandela, *Long Walk to Freedom*, (1994)

First published in the UK in 2023 by The Curious Philomathic.

A CIP catalogue record for this book is available from the British Library.

ISBN 978-1-915955-00-5

Printed and bound by a print on demand service to reduce the impact on the environment. The book is also available as an eBook.

The conversations in the book all come from the author's recollections, though they are not written to represent word-for-word transcripts. Rather, the author has retold them in a way that evokes the feeling and meaning what was said and, in all instances, the essence of the dialogue is accurate.

The names of the characters have also been changed to protect the true identity of each individual within the book.

Dedicated to the bad and ugly for showing me who you really are deep down.

I am forever grateful for the love, belief and support of my wonderful family, not to mention your sacrifices whilst I wrote this book and all the others that are to come.

Special thanks as always go to Lesley, for all her support, guidance and encouragement. This book would not have made it without you.

TABLE OF CONTENTS

INTRODUCTION

Daughter or sister? At the moment of creation I was both and my moral compass should have allowed me to serve both equally? But, if only my roles of playing daughter and sister during this lifetime were as straightforward as that, given the family that I was born into. My role of mother has also come under fire and has presented itself with added complications, needs and wants, and at times, I have felt that I have bowed down to everyone else to keep them happy, while allowing myself to absorb the detrimental effects of those actions.

When dealing with any situation that surrounds gender and sexuality, there is always more than one person involved. Sometimes either party can be blinkered, believing that they are the only people going through the given situation. However, there are always two very distinct and different paths; with both avenues sometimes reaching the same end destination and sometimes going off to different destinations. But both are as valid as the other, so are their stories, thoughts, feelings and journeys along the way. It is unfair for either side to bestow requests on the other; once this happens, it is very hard to pull back from it and separate those positive and negative thoughts. Both avenues should be allowed to have the airtime they deserve, as well as both having the validation they need. In order to help anyone other than oneself, each of us needs to listen, understand and convey their different stories, in order to offer the best support they can. Remembering that no one travels on this journey alone.

Not everyone's journey through transgender family members is like mine, in fact I don't know of anyone with two consecutive generations of transgenders within one family, let alone other family members that are included under the umbrella of LGBTQ+ within the same family. I don't know of any other family that has had so many females to male transition or fit under the LBGTQ+ umbrella in any other way. I wonder if there are any other families in our position? Could there be an argument surrounding family genes? My father's first-born daughter is transgender and my first-born daughter is transgender. My father's first-born son had three children, son, daughter, son. At the time of writing this book, the last time I saw my niece she was eleven years old and was already showing signs of being queer. Many years on, I don't know where she has now ended up but it would not surprise me to hear that she was gay or has even transitioned. I also have a daughter who is lesbian.

To make this clear to readers, because I can appreciate how difficult understanding it all might be, my father married two different women and each of those women had children fifteen years apart. Out of those children, all the females that followed, particularly, all of the first-born daughters or granddaughters have gone on to have gender reassignment surgery or have identified as lesbian. Is it me or is this just a huge coincidence? Could there actually be something contained within my father's genes?

Wouldn't it be exciting to be able to do further scientific research into this and see whether my theory can be backed by scientific evidence? And if it could be backed up, would there then be a further argument for gene selection? If this ever fell into the wrong hands, could scientists effectively wipe out a whole LGBTQ+ community? In effect using ethnic cleansing to change the path of humanity? Would our human rights be even more restricted by power and the mindsets of others?

Only one element is certain, there is more than one person that goes through and deals with transgender. Yes, there is a strong argument for the person transitioning and yes, the main focus should be on that individual. However, aren't we all learning to deal with transitioning? Aren't the people who sit on the side lines transitioning too? The answer is YES. We are dealing with transitioning but in a different way and that too needs to be recognised and appreciated and actually validated that we too have the right to seek help and further understanding, in order to deal with it in the best way possible. Maybe not in the same way but in some way. We are in effect watching our loved ones recreate themselves.

Although we are only watching the outer shell of the person change, I have found that I went through a process of grief for one transitionee but not the other. However, being a part of this process doesn't and shouldn't change the fundamentals of who the transistionee is on the inside, and hopefully it is only the outer packaging which changes, in some cases this is not the case. As loved ones, we already love the person for who they are and will love them even more for the challenges they may have to face head on. We want to see them happy and not suffering. However, anyone going through gender reassignment may insist that they haven't changed. Insisting that it would merely be society and how they perceive gender that will impact them differently in their new outer shell. We will all have to learn to adapt.

Demands are placed on us, which are sometimes not manageable and not achievable. Nevertheless, they are asked of us and we are expected to appease them. I know I have had more than my fair share of requests placed on me which I simply can't deliver. And why should I? I think that they are unreasonable, and I have been left to feel very hurt and confused by some of them.

From a child's point of view, we all have something to complain about when it comes to how our parents raised us or treated us. As a parent, I understand even more so, that when you have a child, a parenting book doesn't just miraculously fall from the sky and land on your lap, there isn't a rule book; most parenting is done by the seat of our pants. There isn't anyone to turn to who has truly mastered the art of parenting, because the long and short of it is, that parenting is parent and child specific. Each situation is different from the one before or the one next door. And each child is different and shouldn't be thought of as a replica of the child before. I would challenge anyone, if they think they could do better in the same situation – by all means give it a go. Hindsight, time, change of circumstances and a different mindset are a human's best and worst friend all rolled up in one from one year, four years, ten years or more down the line. We all have to make a choice at that time and hope for the best.

However …

Having made that choice, we can choose to keep on that path or make the changes necessary to make everything better, right or more manageable.

My life and how I have turned out is all thanks to my mother with the help of my sister and the way they navigated not only transitioning but how they have treated me in general. They have been the driving force behind me, and at the completion of this book I was finally able to understand that I had been in fact gripped in an narcissistic abusive relationship involving verbal and emotional abuse, delivered by the both of them for over forty-two years of my life. With the both of them equally contributing to the abuse and fueling it, and neither of them wishing to stop it. As I sit here, as a mother myself, I am finding it hard to comprehend just how a mother could be so wicked, to play with one life is bad enough, but she played a very calculated game within the circle of abuse with my sister and my own children, while playing the victim to the outside world, portraying me as the bad guy, it is just unforgivable. But, it has helped me become the woman my mother knew she would never be. Strong, independent, resourceful and capable of achieving the things she only talked or dreamt about. But that is a whole different story which will be another book. This book however, will serve as my evidence should I ever want to take the matter further and seek the final closure that I want.

At the time of writing this book, I am a mere forty-three years in age, yet I feel I have lived a lifetime. I have definitely seen a life overflowing with events, twists, turns, love and heartbreak. Yet, I feel my story is only just in the early stages of its beginning. I am only now finding my feet and freedom from my gilded cage and achieving what I have always known I was capable of. In the last forty-three years, I have had to remain silent and invisible and very much under the thumb of my family. However, despite my feelings and the gilded cage, I will always remain respectful of my own children.

We as a family have a story to tell which I hope will lead on to helping others going through something similar. Trying to bring in as many different angles, opinions, facts, thought processes, in order to better equip anyone and everyone to not just helping themselves but those around them too. I think there could be so much more done for all things relating to gender and sexuality and I feel that there is so much more that doesn't get discussed that should be. We need to break the taboo that comes with these conversations and help others to be able to freely discuss how they feel and what their needs are.

I was raised in a family that didn't discuss gender issues or anything to do with sexuality. In fact, my father was very old fashioned, black was black, white was white. He never allowed conversations to happen in the grey zone. However, I am very grateful that I didn't learn from his behaviour and didn't end up with the same attitudes as him. We need to break the cycles of learnt behaviour where we can.

Having come from quite a sheltered upbringing and now navigating through a very diverse family, my attention is drawn to the mental strain that people dealing with gender and sexuality issues go through. How, from this angle there simply isn't enough support out there for them, if they don't have understanding family or friends. Not to mention the emotional and mental strain that family and friends go through. I do also appreciate that in this particular societal group, things are always moving and changing very rapidly. However, some of those changes could be seen as not enough and some of them could be seen as a hinderance too.

Over the years, I have gone through many different scenarios, some self-inflicted, some not. Some I have seen coming and some I was not prepared for at all. But in all that, my life has been in preparation for the story I am about to tell. My journey to reach this point has paved the way to allow me to be the best person I can to help others who have been placed in my care. Their needs, their story, their own evolution has been my primary aim and priority. I have been honoured to help nurture, care and provide a safe space and place for them.

But, as always, there will be some people who disagree. I have learnt to set these people free on their own path. Far from mine and from those I chose to have on it with me. These are the people that are toxic and damaging and no matter how hard that is to deal with and to set free,

I have had to learn to put my family first and do what is best for us all.

No one should have to put up with people who are toxic. None of us deserves that.

PROLOGUE

Normal is a word whose meaning is often defined by our experiences and upbringing. Therefore, its definition can be very personal to each of us. Please consider for a moment what normal means to you and where that definition comes from? As a suggestion, why not write your thoughts down and place them into an envelope before reading my story and revisiting them once you have finished. Do you think your view on the term normal has changed?

The Collins dictionary states, “Something that is normal is usual and ordinary.” Wikipedia states, “Normal can also be used to describe individual behaviour that conforms to the most common behaviour in society.” There are more and more people breaking those barriers of silence and looking for their *normal* label. As more individuals come forward new definitions of normal emerge which define their social and sexual preferences. There are more and more individuals coming forward in whatever way they feel they identify with, but the point is, that there are more people of the same identity coming forward, which means they are defined as normal.

We are all normal human beings, because there is more than one of us that feels the same way. Over the years, society has created this unrealistic version of normal because it was better to follow the herd than not. ‘Upsetting the apple cart’, or ‘breaking from the norm’, all spring to mind from the generation before us and probably within the generation many of us grew up in. We only have to look more deeply at the number of fifty-year-old plus 'heterosexual' couples whose partners have redefined themselves as LGBTQ+ post-divorce and following their children becoming adults and the realisation that they don't have to hide away anymore. Beliefs that were installed in them by their *Collectivism* parents, that they had to marry the 'normal' way and stay together for the children's sake. Or how many 'heterosexual' people who now inhabit unheterosexual dating and hook-up sites whilst pretending to conform to out-dated definitions of normal. We are seeing more and more people openly coming forward to break their own learned behaviour, in order to find happiness and not to live a life as a lie or in the shadows. Proving that what Karl Marx stated in his Contribution to the Critique of Political Economy: "It is not men's' consciousness which determines their being but their social being which determines their consciousness." But, I think society's version of normal is fake and should be exposed for what it is. It's an ideology which makes money from products and services linked to the 'new norm'. It only benefits those people who would try to impose their own blinkered view of what is acceptable. Look at the church and generations of governments; they have surely been more guilty of that than many other groups?

Doesn't the church and government receive funding from wealthy individuals which is often given on the basis of reinforcement of certain ideologies which hold these types of movements back by trying to set the boundaries and punishing those who would break them? The only way we will break this never-ending cycle of corruption is by society changing as a result of movements just like, 'She said' and 'Me too'. All these confinements and constraints are doing is dividing the human race; when we should be working together to find harmony and acceptance.

Society needs to revisit its version of normal and rename it to inclusive. The ideology of inclusive covers everyone, therefore you become a realistic version of *inclusive* aka normal. Society is reborn with a sustainable, diverse and inclusive reality and it is within touching distance of everyone to reach it and find their place in our society, instead of remaining on the outskirts.

If there is anything this world has taught me, it's that there is no normal. No two individuals are the same; no situation is dealt with in the same way. Really the world would be a very bland and boring place without the huge diversity we have. I feel we should all be celebrating that fact, not hating it or turning on it.

PART ONE
A TOXIC TRANSITION…

CHAPTER 1:
THE CHICKEN OR THE EGG...

Given my situation you could argue, which came first: daughter or sister? Either way the situation remains the same. I was born a daughter to my parents in late 1978, to a sibling occupied family. Therefore, I am both. But, if you are to become a sibling, at what point do you as a parent start preparing your existing child(ren) for the arrival of another smaller unknowing human to assume the role of needy child?

There are many parents who don't feel the need to prepare their children for a new arrival. Although I have said previously that there is no right or wrong way, I do question the failure to prepare any child for the imminent arrival of an interloping child. It damages children to an extent that lasts a lifetime. I know; I have been the center of this failure for my whole life.

My parents never prepared my sister for my arrival. At the point when I was born, my sister had lived blissfully as an only child for twenty-two months. As the stay-at-home parent and not quite the sole care giver for my sister at that time, my mother did nothing and I mean nothing to prepare her. We were brought up with Nanny's looking after us instead of our parents putting in the hard work and time that was needed.

On that fateful day in 1978, my parents left the house for three days and left my sister in the care of our grandparents, with no explanation to her of why or what was happening. The, without mention and all of a sudden, my mother arrived back home. Walked through the door and greeted her with an infiltrator, a usurper, a small new person who was going to make her title of only child meaningless, making her an older sibling and putting her to the back of the needy child queue. According to my grandmother, my sister took one look at the small sleeping bundle wrapped in a blanket and cradled in my mother's arms before turning and throwing herself on the floor in a rage. She cried endless floods of tears, thumped her wrists and kicked her legs on the floor, while screaming and wailing as loud as her little lungs could manage.

I recall my grandmother telling me how horrified she was at the sight of my sister's behaviour and her disbelief at how my mother handled it afterwards. My sister's world had shattered before her very eyes. Her solo existence had expired. Unbeknown to me, my fate was sealed from that moment. My mother had done nothing to rectify the situation or even attempt to reintroduce my sister to me once the air had calmed, nor attempt to build any bridges or form a bond. Instead, she contributed to the divide between us, which would only get bigger and bigger as time went on. My mother had her own motives to contributing the rift which didn't become clear until a year before I wrote this book.

In her head, my sister had believed she was destined to be an only child from the minute she existed to the minute she expired. That's how she saw it. That's how she wanted it. And that's what she was determined to achieve.

The age difference between the two of us shows that one of us was far too young and innocent to even comprehend how utterly betrayed and devastated the other felt. But, needless to say, with myself being the innocent one, I paid the price of our parents' failure and spent a lifetime of living at the very brutal end of sibling rivalry.

My early childhood was awful. I was miserable, lonely and an outcast. Hatred and jealousy oozed in my direction from every pore of my sister's body. I spent what seemed an eternity dodging invisible bullets carrying the most explosive poisonous venom from the moment I woke to the moment I slept. Thankfully, my parents had a big enough house, which meant that we had our own bedrooms from the start. Otherwise, I'm fairly certain I wouldn't be here to tell my tale.

Our father ran his own company and would spend most of the week working abroad or in London, we didn't really have him around very much. He was in the prime of his career and had already raised one family before we came along; he didn't feel the need to be around to raise another one. To put that in context, at the age of about eight, the gardener taught me to ride my bike. One could argue that we didn't have a strong male figure in our lives which may or may not have contributed to how things panned out later down the line.

From an early age my sister and I fought. We fought over the most ridiculous things all the time, from dawn to dusk. It was tiring keeping up with it. The majority of our time was spent fighting for our mother's attention, which my sister was hell bent on always being the first to get. She learnt how to be a cunning little fox and she knew exactly how to play the system.

Not only did I get the blame for every fight that was started, every bad word or glance that came towards her but for everything that happened. She knew how to play the victim and how to get me into trouble all the time. She also knew how to pull the guilt strings which connected her to my mother. I was picked on constantly, no matter what I was doing, my sister would make something out of it and turn it to her advantage.

My mother wouldn't allow herself to reason with us, she wouldn't sit and listen to both sides and if there was the odd chance that she did, it was pointless, she would without a shadow of a doubt take my sister's version of events as gospel and mine as lies. Either way I was on the highway to nowhere, so what was the point in fighting it. My mother was too weak-minded to think for herself and form her own opinions and when she did, they were always tainted and never heartfelt; constantly and subconsciously needing to make amends for her failure on that fateful D-Day. Knowing the part she had played in breaking my sister's heart and shattering her little world. She knew deep down that she would always be making amends and justifying my sister's actions, but she never had the courage to admit it; not even to herself.

As the years went on, she got to a point where she believed her version of events and cover ups, because it had grown easier for her to cope with. She would eventually go on to spend the rest of her life making it up to my sister. Being used, being played and being guilt tripped into doing anything my sister wanted her to do; wrapping her round her little fingers at the drop of a pin. I grew conditioned by this way of life and grew to accept being treated this way. Looking back on it, this is the first sign that I was in an abusive relationship with them both. I will explain this in more detail later on in my story.

Sister, how would you define a sister? A best friend? Someone to share your secrets with? Your clothes, your makeup or even your shoes? Someone who you can rely on; who's always got your back? Someone who hugs you when you are sad? Wipes away your tears? Someone who makes you laugh? Or even someone who knows you better than you know yourself? These are what I would class as the core unspoken bonds between sisters or maybe close siblings in general. However, I seemed to have missed the boat when they were handing out these types of sister. I never once had this; I was not even one step close. You can't miss something you never had, but you can always long for it and live in hope that one day it may come.

The words sisters, sisterhood, bond and best friends never even entered our minds, let alone passed our lips. Being left in her company, I was like a lamb to slaughter. Five minutes in a room together was like watching an atomic bomb going off; I didn't have the stomach to stick around and deal with the fallout heading in my direction.

Being born a girl in the 1980s meant only one thing. Frills, florals and pretty girly clothes. We didn't really get a say in what we wore, but I never had an issue with it. I was a girly girl. I did girly things like doing my hair, makeup, nails, dressing up and dancing. It does have to be said that all the above is acceptable to both genders; the gender barrier needs to be broken in more ways than one. Back in the 1980s you were either a girly girl, a man's man, or a tomboy, which meant one thing, or something else which I refuse to label.

I fitted into my girly girl stereotype and the things I liked to do. I was happy with who I was, how I looked and what I did. I had a place and I fitted in. My sister on the other hand, kicked against the frills, the florals and pretty girl clothes. She wanted trousers, short hair and boxer shorts. I remember going for bra fitting at a store called Army and Navy. The lady who attended us was old fashioned, knew her job inside and out and could tell your bra size without you taking your clothes off. My sister hated going, she hated the whole process of bra wearing and getting naked in front of anyone. I never minded, I knew I was coming away with beautiful lacy bras, whereas my sister would come away with plain boring, sports bras. My father struggled constantly with our polar opposites in the clothing department and often came to logger heads with her and my mother about it. Especially, when we had a formal function to attend with our parents. We had it drummed into us from an early age, that our parents moved in certain circles and that we had to conform to those circles. My father refused to be shown up and my sister had no choice but to accept it. When we attended formal events with him, he liked us in matching formal outfits, which represented the indisputable fact that we were girls.

For years my sister's invisible bullets headed in my direction. Her frustration became more and more evident as the years went by. She hated it when we had to go anywhere important. Particularly, when I wore the clothes I was given without complaint and got recognition for it, again that cycle of emotional abuse comes into play too much during my childhood. When all she got was a telling-off; an argument and my mother trying desperately to plead with my father to allow her to wear what she was comfortable in. She always thought I had one up on her because of this and it didn't go down well. At some stage, either later that day or the next, I would always pay the price.

She learnt to vent her frustration and anger towards me and would pick holes in anything and everything I did. Everything I wore, it was ugly or it was yucky. Everything I did was stupid and girly. Every action towards me was filled with hatred and frustration. It wasn't long before she started verbally throwing bullets at me, constantly calling me fat and ugly. Drumming it into me that no one would love me with how I looked.

Her body and how she perceived her role – her place in the world – became more and more untenable throughout our childhood. It became even more unbearable to be in her company. No matter how many times I bit back, which amounted to no more than twice, it never stopped, nor did my mother ever step in to challenge it regardless of being present most of the time. She would always turn a blind eye, which led to my sister having a free rein in her continuing campaign of abuse. She was never reprimanded and it wasn't until I turned forty-two years old, that I finally built up the courage to say, enough was enough.

But it wouldn't be until 2001 when I would finally find out why I had been at the very blunt end of my sister's wrath, it wasn't just about her hatred towards me, there was something else going on with her. Even knowing what I know now, it didn't make it right or more acceptable and I never received the acknowledgement that I needed, which made it even worse. I had been put through years of mental abuse consisting in verbal and emotional abuse, which manifested into eating disorders, drinking, drugs and one hell of a knocked self-confidence, not to mention being an easy target for abusive partners or even abusive children, until I got to the point when I started calling the shots and not allowing it anymore.

You see, not only did my sister have an unconscious underlying hatred and dislike for me, but she was also fighting something that she had no idea about. She hated herself. But I'm not sure who she hated more? It would always be me no matter the circumstances, she oozed hatred from ever pore towards me and I've learnt to accept that. At the end of the day, the issues raised are her issues and not mine. It's taken me a lifetime to realise that and accept it. The problem will always remain her problem and not mine.

CHAPTER 2: **UNRELATABLE…**

Looking back at my childhood and knowing what I know now, makes it all seem so clear. I can pinpoint so much which has helped me to unpick everything; to see it for what it was and still is. To help me come to terms with the fact that it actually wasn't me and it wasn't my fault.

My father's parents had passed away long before we were both born, and my mother's parents had lost their son at the age of sixteen years old. My mother would be their only hope for any future grandchildren. The only person my sister would allow herself to have a relationship with was my mother. She would only allow herself to show and receive affection from her. This must have been a huge blow to other members of the family, especially as she was the first-born grandchild. My sister would do whatever it took to shy away from anyone else who showed any element or level of affection. I wonder whether she instinctively knew she wouldn't be able to play them like she did my mother? Or whether she really was so dependent on the emotional merry-go-round of temper, guilt, soothing and how addictive it had become. Looking back on it, was my sister and mother in some sort of abusive relationship too. When you break down the cycle of abuse, there are four stages – tension, incident, reconciliation and calm, it seems to me that they too were very much stuck on this cycle. I guess I will never truly know, because both of them have lived this way for such a long time that their own judgement and rational way of thinking has become so blurred; they can't see the wood for the trees.

Take my father for instance. My sister didn't have a solid relationship with him. She didn't want to spend time with him nor to have any affection from him or show any towards him. Their relationship was awkward and strained. With three sons from his first marriage, having a daughter was very high on his list of priorities. From his point of view, there must have been an air of excitement, but all he got was disappointment served through her actions. I do appreciate that not all fathers always want or need sons to make them feel accomplished as a father and that they are fathers out there who relish the idea of having daughters. Looking back on it, the rejection must have been very hard for my father to cope with. There is a flip side of course, my father was never really at home very much, we got used to him going away during the weekdays and only being at home at the weekends. Being the age of fifty years old at the time of my birth, he soon tired of doing normal parent things with us and the quality time together never came when he was at home. We never went to the park to play football or go on the swings; we never went on family bike rides and any family holidays we did go on were very much adult driven. We were truly raised to be seen and not heard.

The lack of affection and time spent with my

grandparents can also be said to be the same. She was their first granddaughter. They must have felt hurt and upset when she didn't want to spend time with them or refused to be held, cuddled or even loved by them after that fateful day. I can't' comment on what it was like before I arrived, only from when I did. They must have wondered why though? And I do wonder if they quietly and subconsciously knew something was amiss or not quite right? Later on, my grandfather would be able to find out where and to be a part of the transition process, but sadly my grandmother had left this world before that this time.

I, the polar opposite of my sister, loved my grandparents deeply and I would spend as much time with them as I possibly could. To all intents and purposes, it must have looked as if I was being a goody two shoes and sucking up to them. But in all honesty, I had no one else to turn to. My mother always took the side of my sister, no matter what. In practice the one person, as a child, who I should have felt drawn to and protected by had become useless to me. I didn't feel safe with her because I knew she didn't and wouldn't protect my mental health, which is key to a child's growth. In fact, she contributed greatly to my decline in mental health right up until 2021, when I finally put a stop to it all. Whatever I did, I was always instantly in the wrong. Turning to my grandparents was the only solace I had. They replaced everything that I missed and lacked from both of my parents.

Right from the start, I had a special relationship with my grandparents. I simply adored them and vice versa. If

I could have, I would have spent an eternity with them. Silly things like making apple pies with Granny in the kitchen or trying to find a hidden chocolate stash in the cutlery or linen drawers in the dining room. Or helping Grampy in the allotment area in their garden, watching him tending to his prized runner beans, helping him trim the massive conifers in the front garden. Or sitting with Granny in her sanctuary. We spent an inordinate amount of time together. They were my haven.

On the other hand, my sister never wanted to spend time with either of them, which made it really difficult when we were both left in their care. This created yet another chicken and egg situation. The more time I spent with them and the more I did with them, the more my sister got visibly frustrated at being left out, even though it was only ever her choice not to get involved. But on the other hand, I think she got frustrated at herself for not allowing herself the freedom to join in. I simply couldn't win either way. Was that my fault or was it my sister's? Was it anyone's fault? Could more have been done to protect and nurture the relationship between grandparent and grandchild? Could my mother have stepped in and actually encouraged my sister to do more? Growing up without a grandparent is hard, I know, I have watched my children go through it.

Where did my sister fit in, in all of this?

Nowhere. She didn't have the same relationship with them as I did, and although I was too young to see it or even understand it, it was yet another chink in the armor of hatred and jealousy that came hurtling my way. Just like a hairshirt, I was the irritant to her skin and one she couldn't get rid of.

Our grandfather lived until he was ninety-six years old and it wouldn't be until the last ten years of his life when my sister would spend time with him and build a meaningful relationship with him, which must have been a bitter pill for her.

Whilst I do appreciate how hard it must be to not fully understand why you don't feel like things fit, I can't condone it when someone places their own fears, miscommunications, lack of understanding, whatever label you want to call it, on to someone else. It wasn't my fault. It wasn't something I had done or contributed to. Heck, I did everything I could to stay out of their way. I got chastised for everything that both my sister and mother forced me into. None of it was my doing.

CHAPTER 3: ADOLESCENCE...

The age of eleven years came and went. It was one of the worst years of my life and one that set the tone for the next ten years or more.

With two years between us, I had an extra two years at primary school by myself. I had been looking forward to a longer separation between us, it would mean I could grow my wings and not have to hide in the shadows, fearful of the bullying that I would sustain in front of my friends and hers. She took great pride in picking on me in public, belittling me and making my school life just as much of a misery as it was at home, I couldn't escape her. However, after having two years to myself and by the end of my primary school years, I wasn't banking on what was coming.

My sister had been sent off to an all-girls school twenty minutes down the road for those two years of separation, but when the time came for me to move up into senior school, we were both packed off to separate boarding schools, like a box of shoes being returned. Everything that I knew had gone from underneath me like someone had stood behind me and viciously whipped the carpet from under my feet. I wasn't asked. I wasn't given an option; I was sat down and told I was going. I had no choice in the matter. We were both sent over an hour away from home. No friends or family close by to either of us. We were on our own.

The age of eleven sees the start of adolescence and of becoming a woman and having to deal with all things female. It is also the second most important time in a child's life. I wasn't five minutes down the road, I was over an hour away. I wanted to be at home dealing with that not with a bunch of strangers. To add insult to injury, I was made into a full-time boarder. For those of you who aren't accustomed to boarding school, it meant I lived at school during the whole of term, only coming home for half terms and school holidays. I hated my parents for forcing it on me. I wasn't given a choice or any other alternative. I didn't want to go to that school or any boarding school for that matter and I was never given an option in picking out the next school either. I just had to deal with it.

In the lead up to starting at boarding school, I had to deal with the devastating news that my grandmother had breast cancer. My parents had taken us on holiday to Malta, just to tell us the news. Who takes a child on holiday to tell them that their grandparent or anyone else for that matter is dying. You can't be comforted by them, you can't ask to see them, you have the agonising wait for the holiday to finish and the journey home before you can see them.

Once home, we made the best of the time we had with her, but as always, my mother was the only person going through this journey. She refused to recognise anyone else's pain. Eventually and within six months of starting at boarding school, my grandmother's time had come and I had to deal with the immensity of her loss.

Alone.

It was mid-term and I was allowed to go home for one night, Saturday night. Sunday morning came and I woke up knowing my grandmother had passed away during the night, how I don't know, but I just knew. As I approached the kitchen, I found my mother busy ironing, as I entered, she didn't even lift her head to acknowledge that I was there or to even tell me the news herself. An air of silence was the only confirmation I had, that and opening the fridge door to be greeted with a bottle of champagne chilling on the center shelf. Don't get me wrong, I do fully understand why it was there. When you have watched your loved one suffering like that, the only thing you can do is to celebrate their passing because it means they are no longer in pain. However, my mother was colder than the champagne. She never said a word to me after I had noticed the champagne or even attempted to hug me. The whole house was silent, no one said a word to each other all day. Before I knew it, I was being ushered to pack my things ready for school, so that my father could drive me in silence for a whole hour all the way back to school.

I arrived at school and hurriedly run upstairs to my dorm before heading to assembly, barely time enough to process the events of the short weekend I had had and barely any time at all to process my own loss. That was until, my housemistress came and found me in the middle of evening assembly and told me she was sorry for my loss. Although the words were out of lip service duty, it had been the kindest few words said to me all day, and with that I burst into tears.

It was true, the words that I didn't want to hear, I had lost. I had lost my safety net. Half of the team I could run too, who understood me and saw what I was going through. I had now been effectively thrown into the lion's den. I had nothing to protecting me. As with everything in my life, my mother refused to acknowledge me and how I was feeling. In her mind, she was the only one allowed to grieve, she was the only person going through this awful loss and she was the only one who was dealing with the pain of this loss. No one else could possibly feel how she felt.

Adding grief on an already mentally trodden on young child didn't make for a good mix. It took me the best part of six years to get over and I had lots of ups and downs, lots of rebellious times and butting heads with anyone in authority and more so within my own household. Some would say troubled, but I would say lost and sinking in what seemed an enormous vat of quick sand. Without a shadow of a doubt, my mother didn't equipe me with the tools for dealing with grief, I have had to learn these along the way, and even now I struggle immensely with it.

Within my first eleven short years of life, I had coped with constant hatred and jealousy on a daily basis which was relentless; I had coped with parents who blamed me for everything and anything and who always took sides which were never mine. The feeling of belonging and yet not belonging. And the biggest one of all – grief. Transitioning doesn't have to just relate to transgender. We all have to learn how to transition from one issue or area of life to another. And it's never easy.

There just isn't one person alone who has to cope with transitioning on any level.

1992 brought in my fourteenth year and saw my sister and I shackled together again at the same school. For the love of God. What parent in their right mind would think it a great idea to lock two siblings together for schooling and boarding. Particularly, when there has been a clear, lifelong battle between them? Yet again, we were both full-time boarders, but this time we were even further from home an whole hours drive. I had no escape, nowhere to run to and no one to turn to who knew our background history. My sister had already spent a year at this school, making her own mark. I was just seen as the tag along and as far as the boys were concerned I was expected to follow on from my sister's examples.

It didn't take me long to hear all the rumors about what she got up too with the boys and it didn't take me long to physically witness it either. Like clockwork, you could time her going from one window to another knocking for the sixth form boys to see if they wanted sexual favours and walking off into the woods to fulfil them. This was the behaviour that I was expected to follow. It wouldn't take long for them to realise that I wouldn't be, but when I spoke to my mother about it, she wouldn't hear of it. She wouldn't believe for one moment that her precious daughter would stoop so low.

I do wonder if my parents ever thought that palming us off to someone else to manage would be best all round. Having said that, with the long line of nannies we had, it wouldn't be changing a habit of a lifetime for them. My parents never addressing what went on between us and were at no point willing to help in any way to rectify any damage or put a stop to it. I was left to feel even more disconnected; raw, vulnerable and more of a lamb to slaughter than ever before.

Life at school with my sister was awful. It truly was. One event has stuck with me all my life. I had been bought a bomber jacket from Levi's for my birthday, a blue fabric jacket. I loved it. However, my sister came storming into my room, which I shared with five other girls, and demanded that I gave her my jacket so that she could wear it out. When I told her NO! all hell broke loose. I can remember it as if it were yesterday. I was stood by my bunk bed minding my own business, I turned to see her launching at me, moving at high pace in two large strides and full on rugby tackled me into my wardrobe, leaving me winded and collapsed on the floor, before turning and walking out, throwing my jacket over her shoulder as she went. This was my life rolled up into one defining moment, this was the extent of what I had put up with all my life prior to this and this is what my mother nor father protected me against. I will never forget the look of horror on the other girls faces, when they picked me up off the floor.

Having then phoned home to speak with my mother about it, I had been beaten to it. My sister had got there before me and made up some bullshit, all I got from my mother was, '*Well, you should of just given it to her when she asked.*' There was nothing more I could do. Throughout my schooling years, my brother justified his actions to fellow pupils be telling them it was okay for him to do what he did to me because I was his sister, therefore it gave him the automatic right to do whatever he wanted to me and that no one should or was allowed to step in and stop it.

Looking back on those years at boarding school, I can see now even more clearly how confused, frustrated and desperate my sister was in finding her place or path. And how she frantically tried to make sense of her own issues. One minute she was doing army cadets, parading around with the boys and then playing rugby and fitting in at being as masculine as possible. Then in the next breath wearing dresses and donning thick eye liner and high heels, trying to act as feminine as possible, which never worked. Grace and beauty didn't work in tandem with her. Her awkwardness shined through.

Through all of it, the wedge between us became the size of a canyon with the realisation that it was becoming irreparable and there was no way of salvaging anything that would remotely resemble a sibling relationship. My trust, faith and hope in her were completely diminished. She was toxic and damaging towards me and I didn't want to be a part of this relationship any longer, I kept my head down and out of her way as much as I possible could.

I also had my own issues to deal with, mostly thanks

to her with the reminder thanks to my mother. I had never been given the tools to cope with the loss of my grandmother, so I had turned to drink, drugs and smoking; all mixed in with a side of severe eating disorders. Of course, this lead me to taking the prize of being the bigger disappointment in the family, but nothing was new to me on that front, I was glad to wear the disappointment badge proudly. My father often told me I was the black sheep of the family and not worth the paper my name was written on, so why change a habit of a lifetime. My parents never acknowledged or accepted their own failings, despite me raising them all the time. I do remember my mother trying to take me to counselling but I would never talk. She exhausted so many different counsellors, but when I spoke to her that the issue was her, she never accepted it. In hindsight, I should have spoken out. By today's standards, I should have told someone what life was like at home and that my mother turned a blind eye to everything I was subjected too and even instigated it. But no matter how many times I spoke with my parents about their failings, my words fell on deaf ears and they refused to acknowledge they were in the wrong.

I just had the knack of finding trouble and it sticking to me and me alone. My sister too, was equally as misbehaved at school, she also smoked, drank and did drugs and was the school bike, yet she never got caught and when I tried telling my parents that they couldn't punish me for getting caught when my sister did everything and worse it was never even listened too. My sister was the golden child and couldn't possibly do anything wrong. In the end I thought, well, if I'm going to get blamed for it, I might as well do it.

GCSE's came and went, which meant a welcome relief for me. It saw the two of us finally separated. She went off to a university in Wales and I could either stay where I was or move. I needed a fresh start, so I chose to move. I ended up going to a school in Ascot to do my A level's. The move from West Sussex to Surrey was probably the best thing for me. I did the first half of a school year and never went back. I never went home either. At the age of seventeen, I left home and found work. I found my independence away from a controlling mother and a bully of a sister. There was nothing for me at home, so why stay! By this point, we as a family had drifted further apart. My parent's focused on their golden child and I just got on with life the best way I knew how. I didn't want to rely on them a moment longer than I had too.

Months down the line, whilst my sister was at university, I heard via my mother that she had got a girlfriend. Well, that didn't come as a surprise to me, but it didn't go down well with my father and it took him quite a while to come round to the idea. Coming from the late 1920s really didn't help his perception of a modern way of life. My mother kept it a secret from him for some time and even after the news broke my father refused to allow anyone outside of the family to know.

Back in the 80s-90s, LGBTQ+ was not an issue raised as freely or easily as it is today. Our parents came from a generation that brushed anything and everything that wasn't normal, totally and utterly under the carpet. My father in particular was strict and moved in circles within his business world that he thought would disown him. He literally couldn't afford for that to happen, so everything had to be kept hush hush.

It was no surprise to me though, my sister had always been a tomboy, out roughing it up with the boys, never wanting to acknowledge the need for clothes which were considered to be better suited to the gender she was assigned at birth, or carrying out functions which were considered ladylike. She always had to prove a point, that she was able and capable of doing anything a male could do. She always had to overpower you in some way which I think about now as her underlying mental state of emotional abuse. She would constantly competing against anyone and anything just to prove that point, always making her mark on the world. But at last, my sister had seemed to find some peace. Some happiness. She seemed comfortable in her own skin, which was a first in all those years.

Sadly though, it didn't change her behaviour towards me, despite my slight hope that things would change. My hopes were dashed within the first five minutes of meeting up again. I think that the underlying way she felt about me was so ingrained that whatever happened within her own life was certain to never change how she was with me. The odd times I did go back home, we fought like hell. I couldn't bear to be in her company or with parents who never put a stop to her hate-filled behaviour. Turning a blind eye, brushing under the carpet and not appearing to hear the vile comments and never challenging them. Somehow both my parents appeared deaf at the exact same time.

I either accepted it and grew thicker skin to cope with it or I walked away.

I chose the latter.

CHAPTER 4: **THE START OF ADULTHOOD...**

The canyon forged during our adolescence grew wider as we both grew into our roles as adults and led very different lives. We had less and less to do with each other than ever before. No phone calls to ask how the other was, no jokey texts between siblings, no arranging to meet up or to plan a surprise visit to our parents. Our existence as siblings was only on paper. I very rarely went home. I was seen as the child who had abandoned both her parents and the term *family*. And to be honest I didn't really care much. I was happy being out of such a toxic environment.

However, and it is a massive however and also most probably the biggest contradiction going. At nineteen, I was embarking on getting married. My parents hadn't been there to support me at any other time in my life, yet they wanted to fund my wedding and pull out all the stops regardless of what I said or wanted.

I had been dating a landscape gardener for some time and it seemed like the next step. He came from a different upbringing from mine. A much bigger and closer family than I had been used too. Nevertheless, I had been welcomed with open arms. Dean had three siblings, one sister and two brothers; sadly one brother had passed when Dean was seventeen years old, but he had many aunts and uncles. His sister and brother were already married and had children already or children on the way. Our first meeting with both sets of parents to discuss the wedding, didn't go as we had planned. As I found out later, Dean's parents realised how stuck up my parents were and how out of place they felt. My parents refused any offer of financial input, despite Dean's parents wanting to share the cost of what was turning out to be such an extravagant wedding, because of their pride. It was a disaster. But, out of all the chaos, they did notice that life wasn't as happy as my parents tried to pretend. Dean's mother was quick to spot the tension between my mother and I. And how she changed when my sister entered a room. The look my future mother-in-law threw me and her look of disbelief, made me realise that it wasn't all in my head.

Little did I know that my parents wanted to use the wedding to their own advantage and that it would be done their way regardless. My mother commandeered my wedding from the start and by the end she had taken over entirely. The only thing I had a say in, was my own dress. At different points throughout the preparations, I had thought about running off and getting married. Just the two of us, but dealing with the ramifications wouldn't have been worth it. My father was too strict and old fashioned, I had already filled my quota of disappointment with him, because I didn't live up to what he expected. As far as he was concerned, I broke the boundaries all the time, I wouldn't of been surprised if he asked for a black sheep to be present at the wedding, least of walk me down the aisle. Living with this level of disappointment can be very hard. I wasn't about to add to it. So, for once, I towed the line.

I was adamant that I didn't want my sister to be my bridesmaid. She hadn't earnt that right in all the time we had been sisters. Unsurprisingly, my mother had other ideas though and wouldn't hear of anything other than her being my bridesmaid. My sister had gone kicking and screaming to anyone who would listen, making me out to be the big bad sister who was refusing her a prime place at the head of the wedding. Too bloody right I was. My father had turned a blind eye and didn't want to get involved; he had other things on his mind. I had no one to back my corner; to be a mediator. In the end, my mother had utterly betrayed me by forcing my tyrant of a sister – someone who was truly unworthy of the role – upon me.

Many of you reading this may think that was harsh of me, but if you had lived a life in the shadows, watching your sister getting everything she wanted, twisting both parents round her little finger and making you out to be the villain, whilst showing you her hatred and jealousy at every waking moment. Bullying you from the moment you woke to the moment you slept and who made your life a true misery, then you might then feel the same. She didn't deserve to have that title or role in what should have been one of the most important days of anyone's life. Yes, there could have been an opportunity to reconcile whatever was going on between us. But having tried that on more than a handful of occasions, I already knew from experience that I was not only wasting my time and emotions not to mention hope, but it would be a fruitless exercise. It takes two to make it right and if one party is not willing to step up, then what's the point. As with many events in my life, my sister did her best to either upstage me or manage to achieve ruining whatever it was that I was doing.

It didn't stop there. Metaphorically, she had got her foot wedged firmly in the door and she wasn't going to move it for anyone. It was meant to be my wedding, yet my sister managed to call the shots. Firstly, she didn't want to wear a dress; she didn't want to play that part not even for just one day. Secondly, she wanted to wear what she wanted, which happened to be a black tuxedo.

I was having a traditional Celtic themed wedding. Coming from a Scottish background, I wanted to enhance the colours of our family's tartan against the amazing backdrop of Amberly Castle. Naturally I didn't agree to her choice of outfit. A black tuxedo for a bridesmaid. Why would I? It wasn't even going to match the colour theme. Not to mention that she would look out of place – be an eyesore. Not that she liked me telling her to her face, her petulant child came out again and she stomped off to our mother to sort me out. If her choice of outfit had been a smart tailored suit in a different colour that would have been acceptable. My father and other brothers were wearing the family tartan and the remaining guests were in morning suits. At what possible juncture does a black tuxedo fit in with this theme?

In the end, we both had to compromise. My mother wasn't prepared to fight my corner and I became exhausted with waiting and expecting her to actually consider putting me first. She wanted my sister as my bridesmaid. My sister demanded to be a bridesmaid and that was that. In the end, it was agreed that she would wear an understated and very plain purple floor length dress, which showcased her horrendous and tacky tattoos from university days. She would also still end up being my bridesmaid.

Does my distain show?!

I was allowed to have one friend to attend my wedding, the rest of the people attending were at the request of my parents. Each and every one of them had something to do with them but not with me. It was a show of my parents wealth to their friends, it wasn't a day about me. Included among their friends and unbeknownst to me at the time, my father's mistress! She was the cleaner ay my parent's home and had spent ten years measuring up her life against my mother's and she was determined to get her claws into my father.

I hadn't planned on having a hen do, I hadn't even named a matron of honor but it would have been nice for someone to actually think of me. A long shot I know! Not even my mother or sister felt the need to throw me a hen do for me. In all honesty the thought of spending a drunken night with them as well as my future husband's sister and sister-in-law filled me with even more dread than the wedding itself. Nevertheless, it would have been nice for one of them to at least arrange something. But instead, and whoopee – lucky me – I spent the night before my wedding with them both in the same room. The whole night consisted of going to bed and waking up.

It would be some years after my wedding when my sister got married. At no time was I ever put on her list and considered for the role as her bridesmaid. Nor was my mother willing to fight my corner to allow me to be her bridesmaid. I was relegated to being an Usher. I role I didn't fulfil and gladly took my own place on a seat. Funny that!

Not long after my wedding had come and gone, my sister and I resumed our roles of paper-only-sisters and parted company. I had nothing more to do with her and kept my distance as much as possible. My mother and father divorced soon after my wedding, which as an adult was quite hard to cope with. Again, my mother was the only person who was going through the grief of the situation, she was the only one involved. Especially, once. The divorce brought in a change within our family and not wanting to go into too much detail, but it was the last time I saw my father or had any other contact with him. I was stuck between a rock and a hard place. My mother, let's not forget that I really didn't owe her anything, felt that she couldn't turn to my sister for help. So she asked for my help and because of my assistance I lost my father. Whether my mother knew what would happen, I will never know but I sacrificed my father for her. From my point of view, the divorce brought a huge amount of bitterness from my mother, bitterness she never let go of and which moulded her thereafter, even more so towards me.

At the age of twenty-one I welcomed my first son, Arron, into the world. He wasn't the first grandchild. My older brothers form my father's first marriage, had managed to have five children between them, but sadly we very rarely saw them. They kept their distance from us because of the hurt my mother had caused their mother over twenty years prior. They had already been through one divorce before and they didn't want to go through another one. It brought too many bad memories back for them. My sister and I grew up knowing our brothers as our uncles, because my father thought it best. Unfortunately, I can't answer for him or even enlighten myself or anyone else on that thought process; all I know is that my mother was complicit and went along with it. Willing, not thinking of any possible ramifications for later life.

However, my son was my mother's first grandchild and she had all the glory to herself without having to share it with my father. After their divorce, he moved to the Isle of Wight with his new bride, to set up home with her. He wasn't interested in playing the doting father or grandfather. At the age of seventy plus I'm surprised he was able to play the doting anything …

I had gone my whole pregnancy without my sister's or mother's involvement. I went shopping on my own more often than not, although I had offers to accompany me from my mother-in-law, which I did take her up on. She would delicately talk to me about how much my mother had done to help and would show her distain when I would say, not much and just shrug my shoulders; trying to avoid the awkward questions. My mother-in-law had a strong relationship with her daughter and couldn't understand why my mother didn't want to know me or have any form of decent relationship with me. Especially with this baby being her first grandchild. By this point my child would have been my in-law's third grandchild and she was just as excited as when she welcomed her first. I decorated the nursery with the help of my father-in-law who taught me to wallpaper, for which I am eternally grateful for. Again, he pointed out the lack of input from my mother. I also attended all routine appointments on my own apart from the important ones, when my husband would join me. All of which was without any extra support from my mother.

My first pregnancy had been a hard pregnancy, for one reason or another. Mainly because I had spent ten years with eating disorders as a result of my sister's behaviour and with daily verbal abuse from her telling me that I was fat and ugly and that no one would love me. The last thing I wanted was for the child growing inside me to be harmed or exposed to any of their toxicity in any way. I ended up overcompensating and eating more than I should have, which in turn gave my sister the power to poke fun at me even more. But that wasn't the reason why I had a hard pregnancy, I ended up with pre-eclampsia and obstetric-cholestasis, which is very unpleasant. I had planned for a home birth but because of my complications, I ended up needing to go into hospital.

Despite not seeing my sister very often, she would always somehow just happen to be at my mother's house at the same time as me, completely unintentionally from my aspect. Or she would invite herself along with my mother on the odd occasions when she paid me a visit. Either way it was inevitable that I would see her, whether I wanted to or not. At no point did my mother step in and reprimand my sister. Of all the things to do or say to a pregnant woman, telling them they are fat is not one of them.

CHAPTER 5: **MOTHERHOOD AND BEYOND…**

Although I have one solitary photograph of my sister and my first son, Arron, when he was new-born, that was the extent of their relationship. She had nothing more to do with him than holding him in that photo. The role of aunty didn't exist, and it was clear that having children was considered one of the dirtiest things in her eyes. She couldn't imagine performing the act of sex and then having this thing growing inside of you and one day having to go through the act of giving birth to it. But, despite all my feelings and the way I had been treated in the past, I had always offered to be a surrogate for her should she ever want to become a mother. It wasn't until a lot later down the years when I found out from my mother that my sister didn't think I was good enough to be used as a donor for either eggs or to be a carrier. There is nothing else I can add to that sentence. Cuts like a knife just doesn't even come close.

Having children and being a mother was something I had wanted to do since I was a young girl. I loved being pregnant; I loved carrying a growing baby inside me and watching my bump grow. Compared to my difficult first pregnancy, I was incredibly lucky and managed labor with relative ease. I loved breastfeeding and managed to do so for an extended period of time. I loved being a mum. If I could have, I would have happily been a surrogate for anyone who was unable to carry a child, without recompense, whether they were my own children or friends. How can you put a price on giving life, love and enjoyment to another human.

By 2001, I was expecting another child and I had learnt from my mother's failings not to make the same mistake as she had. I had introduced my first child to the prospect of having another smaller human in the family right from the moment I found out I was expecting. He accompanied me to all of my appointments; all of my scans and he even came shopping with me, helping me to pick out outfits and teddies etc. He was there to help decorate the new nursery and to pick out the gift he was going to give to his new brother or sister. He was included in anything and everything.

Three weeks and three days before his second birthday, I gave birth to my second child. I had planned for a home birth this time round despite ending up with obstetric-cholestasis again, which I was able to have this time round. Meaning that although my first child was only two years old, I was able to give him his last breastfeed and put him to bed. We talked while I feed him at the prospect of him waking up to a new addition and he knew he would be greeting his long-awaited sibling.

We weren't able to find out the gender of our second baby, purely because every time we went for a scan, the baby always seemed to be lying in the wrong position, no matter how hard the sonographer tried to move them around. It's not that we didn't want to find out, we just couldn't. I think in the back of my mind I always knew I was having a girl though. I didn't suffer with any morning sickness like I did with my first. And, not that movement was anything to go by, my second baby didn't move as much and seemed calmer while in utero. So, when I went into labour and the baby decided to make a grand entrance, it came a shock. It was one hell of an entrance; forty-five minutes to be precise, from start to finish.

I couldn't have asked for it to be more perfect. I have the photograph showing my two year old's little face at the excitement of greeting his baby sibling the next morning. They were inseparable. All my hard work had paid off.

My second child was born at a really difficult time. Our marriage wasn't great and we had spent many months at dis-ease, which can takes its toll. Mentally, I was all over the place plus I had struggled with the same medical complications as with my first pregnancy and I had worried myself sick with everything. Needless to say, I was exhausted by the time I had her. Two little ones to deal with plus focusing on repairing and concentrating on a marriage, felt like a constant juggling act.

I needed time to heal both physically and mentally with everything I had going on. But, regardless of that, my mother, being someone who was totally incapable of reading someone else's feelings and only ever putting herself first, in her ultimate wisdom paid me a visit just seven weeks after having my baby, late on Christmas Eve. It wasn't the first visit she had paid since her birth, but because I had stood my ground and told her that I wouldn't be dragging our children out on Christmas morning, she had decided she would just pop round uninvited. True to form and only thinking of herself, she ploughed her way through the front door and swiftly sat on the sofa, half on half off, I don't think she even took her coat off, which was a dead giveaway that she wasn't planning to stay longer than she had too. She had never liked staying in my home for any more time than she needed too.

There was no beating about the bush, she got straight to the point, no asking how we were or whether we needed anything or whether we were ready for Christmas. She started off the conversation after an awkward silence, dropping in the words transition, change, not gay, all muddled into one sentence. By the end of it, I sat there totally confused and not understanding a word she'd said, all the while trying to feed a crying baby and listen to her. The louder the baby cried over her the more she seemed to get frustrated, and because I was preoccupied, I didn't understand a word of what she was trying to tell me. Not forgetting that we were raised in a household that didn't talk about topics like this. Effectively, we had a sheltered life, so why would I understand her when what she was saying to me came out as a garbled mess? My mother got even more frustrated at me when she had to slow down and explain step by step. Eventually, she spelt it out; my sister was preparing to transition from female to male. My sister had finally worked out what was different about her and what she needed to do to correct it. And that was that. Up she got from the sofa, turned to me and told me to have a lovely Christmas and then she left. As I have already mentioned my mother gave equipped me with emotional tools for dealing with difficult subjects and freely express myself in a way that I needed to.

Talk about being put through the emotional wringer and the mixed emotions from her announcement hitting me like a cannon ball square in the face. What the hell was I meant to do with information like that! Can you not see everything that I was dealing with? Or am I just in just invisible to you?

Once I finally got my head around it, well that explains that then! The actions towards me and to everyone else, the hating herself and me, the clothes, the things she did, how she acted or conducted herself, etc. I had so much going through my head. But it was clear, it was all about my sister and my mother. She had now become my mother's sole priority, foxtrot oscar to anyone else that gets in the way.

No, I totally and one hundred percent didn't take the news well. I struggled massively with it. It left me feeling more wound up than a clockwork toy.

In hindsight, I wouldn't change how I handled it. And no, I don't regret the way I handled it. For one simple reason. My sister had put me through hell for over twenty-two years. I had been bullied, picked on, beaten, laughed at, mentally damaged and all on a daily basis, I wore the scars to prove it, both mentally and externally. All while the added pressure of dealing with being ostracised from my family because of her.

I wanted recognition, for what I had been through as a result of her deep hatred of herself for all those years. I couldn't work out why, but I wanted my family to recognise what I had been through, that I had been wronged and that it actually wasn't my fault. To have my feelings validated in the same way she was demanding to have hers validated. And I wanted to know why I wasn't allowed my feelings. Why wasn't I as important as her. Why didn't my mother see my pain and why wouldn't she acknowledge it? My sister had always hated the fact that I was okay with myself, that I fitted in.

I wanted my mother to stand in front of me and tell me she now understood and recognised what I had been through and how sorry she was for not seeing it and helping to put a stop to it. I wanted my mother to love me in the same way she loved my sister. To even look at me in the same way. But she didn't. She walked out the door as though this news was like water off a duck's back and without any care for my feelings. She couldn't get out of the door fast enough.

I thought about all of the things I had put up with, the pain, the hurt, the relentless verbal abuse. The words that had been spoken to me over and over again, I was fat, I was ugly, no one would love me. It wasn't just the abuse from my sister, I had put up with an equal amount from my mother too, as well as neglect, emotional neglect. Everything that I had been put through for over twenty-two years. That night, I cried myself to sleep, mourning for a sister I never had and for a sister that I had grown to hate. I mourned for the sister I never knew and I mourned for the sister who was no longer. I won't lie, the timing was not the best for personal reasons. I still had so much to work out with my husband, We'd just had another baby and it was Christmas; the level of stress on my shoulders was already immense.

Despite my husband trying to be as supportive as possible, this was uncharted territory for both of us. I had never dealt with anything of this magnitude, nor did I even think it was possible. Transitioning at the turn of this century was still in its infant stages. I couldn't even imagine how the world was going to perceive her. I had never heard of it, I had never even read it, let alone know any of the procedures.

I do thank God for sending me the children, I threw myself into being a mother even more so and turned my focus to them. I remember talking with my in-laws and I can still remember their reaction, "Well, why would she want to do that?" A dumbfounded look had come across their faces. They had even less understanding of it than I did, and couldn't work out why anyone would or even could go through it.

In my way and in the only way I knew how to cope with anything painful, to exercise my feelings, I wrote them down. To this day, no matter how jumbled, I get my thoughts down on paper. It helps me to make sense and gain clarity. It helps me process my thoughts and make some sense.

The next day, I sat and wrote a letter to my sister, telling her how proud I was that she had recognised what she needed to do, but that I couldn't be a part of it. I didn't want to be a part of it and I couldn't cope with being a part of it. I couldn't watch this person who had bullied me my whole life transform without even the smallest acknowledgement towards me. I couldn't just forget what I had been subjected too and live in hope that the new outer shell was going to erase everything. That this sudden change was going to bring about someone with a different mindset and conscience.

Sadly, it doesn't work like that. Some people may say that I am the one who has come across as being selfish and only thinking of myself. Rightly so, no one else was going to do it for me.

I didn't see my mother all over Christmas, the letter was sent after Boxing Day and she had already shown her resentment at the fact that I wanted to stay in my own home spending these precious moments with my children. I didn't want to have to perform like a monkey for her and I certainly didn't want to be the subject of my sister's abuse in front of other people.

By writing the letter and sending it when I did, I fell right into a trap. A trap I hadn't even seen coming, and one I wouldn't understand until now, more than twenty years later. This letter was all my sister needed. It gave her everything she had ever wanted, my mother! Our mother wasn't going to choose between the two of us. Not that any parent should choose between their children. But my mother had already spent half my lifetime putting my sister first.

With her refusal to acknowledge even slightly what I had gone through, my mother also fell into the twisted trap. My sister had won. True to form, she had my mother all to herself.

My mother effectively cut me off from the family. She didn't even put a support package in place for me, she didn't even ask how I was or how I was coping. Finally, I was excluded from the family in everything and anything. It was all about my sister. My mother wasn't going to stand there and have anyone kick up against what was going to happen. I was collateral damage. Damage she readily tossed to the roadside.

Or so I thought. It turned out that it was about both of them.

My mother loved and I mean loved to the point of craving, all the extra attention that came her way. The explaining she had to do over and over again to anyone willing enough or listen or ask. Playing the devoted mother to a child in need. How hard it must have been losing a daughter but gaining a son. And discussing with anyone that would listen, how she'd been there night and day catering for his slightest needs. She would go as far as to say that she always knew he was meant to be a boy because of how he kicked in her tummy, when she was expecting him. She even believed in the excuse she gave about his behaviour and actions prior to his transition. Have you ever heard anything so ridiculous?

Not once, did she ever mention me, she denied my very existence. Not once was I ever asked after. My mother had effectively brushed me and my existence under the carpet. Out of sight, out of mind. She had even gone as far as to have all the photographs of me removed from the house, so that no one would ever ask who the person in the photos was.

Through all this change and family turmoil, the one person who was unchanged, it was my grandfather, he was amazing. He had just turned ninety and had seen a lifetime of change coming from the 1910s, but he took it all in his stride.

At the astounding age of ninety-one, my grandfather proved that you don't have to be a product of your upbringing. He coped with the transition brilliantly and effortlessly and most certainly put my efforts to handle it to shame. Although, I had very different reasons why I didn't handle it, which he knew about. I do believe that out of all of our family members, he always knew that something like this was going to happen. The whole process never fazed him. He just wanted to see his family happy; in whatever shape or form that meant.

My grandfather wasn't the only male in the family, there was also my father and despite his disappearance and abandonment of his family, he had to be told at some point. Many years down the line, I had found out that my brother had been secretly receiving letters from my father. My mother also knew and they never told me. Once my brother had told him about the gender reassignment, my father's communication intensified and he had invited him to stay with them on the Isle of Wight, providing he never told me. My father always said to me, "I wasn't worth the paper my name was written on." I guess he did truly mean it.

CHAPTER 6:
TIME GOES BY…

All my life I have learnt to survive by myself, depend on myself and trust no one but myself. At some points throughout my life, it has been really hard to just survive alone and at some points, I never thought I'd make it. But I have the view, you can't miss something that you've never had and I never had a mother who was there for me, I never had a mother to protect me, so why change a habit of a lifetime? Why put myself through looking for that support from her any more.

I have already mentioned that I didn't and couldn't cope with my sister's transition and some may feel that I was selfish or ignorant. I would one hundred per cent agree with you. I was selfish. I had to be. No one else fully understood what I was going through, other than my husband. No one else was living surrounded by the hurt and rejection of my childhood. I was the only one looking out for my mental health and I had to protect it at whatever cost. If you had walked my life in my shoes, I would put a bet on it that you would do the very same thing.

And here's my point.

In 2006, some four years after the initial shock, I was faced with a situation I never thought I would have to deal with. I was forced to deal with it and I wasn't given any breathing room.

My third child was born in 2005. All three children had the privilege of having their first photographs taken with their beloved great grandfather – my grandfather – on the day they were born. The apple of my eye; the man I held so much love and respect for. I simply cherished him. He loved the role of being a great-grandfather, the look on his face when he was interacting with them especially with all the different ages. He loved sitting in his armchair with a babe in arms, cooing over them. But equally he loved talking to the older children about his time as a child in the Victorian era.

Sitting round the kitchen table on Christmas Eve 2005, just him and I, deep in conversation about everything and anything, he leant towards me and simply said, "I'm ready." He and my grandmother had been together nearly sixty years at the time of her passing and he had lived nearly twenty years without her. It was no wonder he was ready, it was his time and I wasn't surprised one bit.

"I know you are Gramps," was the only reply I could muster. Regardless of how I felt and how selfish I wanted to be, deep down, I knew, but I didn't let it show in my face. I didn't want him to see how deep my pain at the thought of losing him was. We laughed and joked and said our goodbyes, followed by a long, heartfelt embrace.

That was the last normal memory I have of my grandfather.

As with all elderly people, they seem to have the desire and will to see Christmas in and then it all goes downhill from there.

Boxing day came and went and somehow, he managed to go down with a chest infection, which he hadn't had two days prior. It saw him land himself in hospital, having tests and God knows what.

My mother didn't tell me how ill he actually was and kept telling me there was no need to come to the hospital. Two weeks passed and against my better judgement, having spent those two weeks respecting what she had told me; I made my way into hospital with a sinking feeling in the pit of my tummy. It was now or never.

After I parked at the hospital car park, I sat for a moment, trying to compose myself. Carrying my nine-month-old son, I made my way to the front of the hospital. I had a feeling that I knew what I was heading into. As I walked up the long, long corridor, gripping my baby, I knew I would be facing my dying grandfather and I couldn't escape it even if I wanted too. It was my worst nightmare, but what I didn't count on was having to face my brother at the same time. My mother never once told me he was going to be there.

My mother knew I was coming, I had phoned her beforehand. She knew who else was there with her at the hospital and she knew I would be seeing my brother for the first time because I hadn't seen him during those four years of his transition. They both knew I hadn't seen him during this time too, but it didn't even occur to them. The last time I had seen him he was very much still my sister.

I hadn't been a part of the process. I hadn't been there through each of the stages. I hadn't seen or been a part of any personal transformation or progress, if indeed there had been any.

As I turned the corner into the open ward, I caught the outline of my brother, sat at the foot of my grandfather's bed. All I could focus on was my grandfather and how tiny he looked in the bed, hooked up to lots of machines, with wires coming out of him in all directions. My mother saw me enter, she mutter quietly under her breath to my brother and looked me square in the eyes. My grip on my son tightened, it was like a physical blow to my chest, she had lied to me. I was emotionally winded. Neither my mother nor my brother showed me one ounce of respect, by leaving or allowing me to spend some time with my grandfather one on one, nor by telling me in advance that my brother would be at the hospital, nor even the state of my grandfather's health. The last time I had spoken with my mother, she had told me my grandfather was conscious, he clearly wasn't. He was in fact in a deep coma; it was only a matter of time now.

How is anyone meant to deal with this level of sensory overload? Let me tell you, it was one of the biggest overloads I have ever had to deal with. I literally had no time at all to work out who was more important, me, my grandfather, my brother, or the babe in my arms? It hit me clearly, at that moment in time my grandfather was the only person that was coming first.

From the bottom of my soles, I managed to find the strength to face what was right in front of me and I managed to remain composed. God alone knows how I managed it, but I did. I headed straight to the top of the bed, grabbed his hand and squeezed it while leaning over to kiss his forehead. He was all I was going to focus on.

Even though he was in and out of consciousness, he knew I was there. He twitched his hand and a smile came from the corner of his mouth, small enough for me to notice as I stood over him. Not much, but it told me he knew I was there. He squeezed my hand.

During those two long weeks, whilst he had been totally conscious and lucid, he must have thought I was awful for not visiting him. He must have thought I didn't love him. What's more, I never got to tell him how sorry I was for not listening to my gut instinct and just coming sooner. I never got to tell him that his own daughter had prevented me from coming to his bedside. She had stripped me from being there with him and she knew it.

That was it, those miniscule moments were all I had with him, they amounted to just over an hour. Before I could compute it, visiting time was over and we had to leave.

I asked if I could come back at the evening visiting time and sit with him once the children were in bed, but I was told I couldn't. My mother made all the excuses possible to say that only my brother was allowed to be there. It wasn't my place to be there. So, I never went back.

My mother phoned me the following morning to inform me that in the small hours, Grampy had died with just my brother for company. Not even my mother had been there for him. All those years when we were growing up and my brother had not wanted to know him. Yet, in the four short years he had with him, he struggled to reclaim a relationship that even mimicked what I had.

For that I pity my brother, I didn't need to be there watching my grandfather taking his last breath to feel connected to him, I had already spent a lifetime doing that. My brother doesn't hold and will never hold the cherished memories I have of a wonderful grandfather. He didn't want to have a relationship with his grandfather when he was growing up. As a result, he missed out on the very best of our grandfather. He let his emotions complicate and halt any form of attachment to anyone other than my mother. I had these wonderful, cherished and precious years with him and I hold on to those in my darkest times. I had the best of him.

CHAPTER 7: A LEOPARD NEVER CHANGES ITS SPOTS...

Having learnt how to navigate grief all over again and with the shock of losing my grandfather, I slowly came to accept my brother. It was not that I had to accept my brother, the person underneath was still the same. It was a case of accepting the new outer appearance when you haven't been a part of that transition process. He was now the only male left from our side of the family. He connected me and himself to our past. And by accepting him, it allowed me access to the family fold once again. Nothing had changed in that respect though; it was like I had never been away. My brother instantly picked up where he left off and the cycle of abuse started all over again. He is the nowadays version of Henry VIII, a tyrant, a selfish, abusive, gluttonous, coldhearted tyrant.

I didn't ask questions, I didn't want to know anything, I just lived in hope that things would have changed enough for us to make the most of the small family we had left, my mother, brother and myself, not including my own family.

All I knew was that he'd had a double mastectomy and that my mother had been present at his bedside, tending to his every need and never left it. He had then gone on to Switzerland to have reconstruction surgery from the skin graft taken from his forearm, some months on from the mastectomy. At that time, Switzerland was the only place pioneering this type of surgery.

I think one of the most difficult emotions I have had to cope with and one of the bitterest pills to swallow and one which has been constantly smeared in my face, was seeing all the photographs strewn on every surface in my mother's house with the three of them, my grandfather, my mother and my brother. I won't lie or pretend that it didn't cut like a knife. I was never once asked if I would like to be included. Or if I ever wanted to have a set of photos with myself and my children.

All those instances when I had asked, even begged my mother and gone so far as to arrange for photos to be taken with me and my children and my mother would always make up an excuse and cancel right at the last minute. On three separate occasions, I had made arrangements and all were cancelled. Towards the end I gave up because I knew she would keep on doing it. So, what was the point.

I don't have any formal or informal photographs of me with my grandfather in his later life. Knowing that the end was coming closer, I had wanted to capture as many memories as possible not just for me, but for my children too. It's not every day you can boast that you've got a great-grandparent. But my mother had other ideas and stole those opportunities and denied me and my children the right to have them. Yet another brick in the great wall of defense I was building around myself.

What made it worse was the knowledge that she had

removed every last detail of me and my children – her own and only daughter and grandchildren – from her home. All the photographs of us had gone. She had put them in the spare bedroom wardrobe, not even face up I might add, they were turned in on each other. Just as if we didn't exist. She effectively denied the fact that she had a daughter or any grandchildren.

I remember being out on a walk with her and the dogs sometime in the later years and we bumped into one of her friend/neighbour that she saw on a regular basis. They asked who I was and it was only then that my mother introduced me as her daughter after scrabbling for words, quickly realising that she was about to be found out by me. The look of shocked horror on this person's face was the equivalent of a thousand words. She removed all traces of me from her life.

Despite yet another hurdle of rejection, my brother and I were finally able to bear to spend more than five minutes in one room and under one roof. Well, I say my brother and I, but I really mean I. I had grown up somewhat and had matured into a different way of thinking. Becoming a mother, had taught me patience and that's how I viewed him, as a child. Progress, no matter how small, is still progress. No matter how short lived it was.

By this point, my brother had fully transitioned. The whole kit and caboodle. There is no denying that it was the right choice for him, physically and mentally. It was just unfortunate that transitioning didn't bring about a better personality and open his eyes to what he had done or how he treated any other human, not just me. The bottom line is, you can try and patch something up, but unless you are willing to invest in fixing everything, repair work no matter how big or small will only ever remain repair work.

I would like to say that his outlook towards everyone changed but I truly know it didn't. Somehow, I was expecting a miracle. He still oozed hatred and jealousy towards me. My very existence brought the worst out in him. He still fought like a petulant child for our mother's attention and demanded to be listened to. It was exhausting being around him. We were adults now, not children fighting in a playground. Looking back as I draft this book, it is evident that my brother had still not addressed any of his deep-rooted emotional issues. He may well have covered over some of the problems with gender reassignment but nothing underlying had been addressed. He looked down on everyone and considered the below or beneath himself, he never accepted any element of fault if something was wrong and he had caused it, he constantly shifted the blame from himself to others around him. To this day he struggles with constantly racking up vast amounts of debt, which my mother continually pays off for him, whilst he secretly gambles and has now ended up on anti-depressants. If these underlying issues aren't properly dealt with, then what hope does anyone – most of all himself – have of living in harmony?

Not long after my grandfather's funeral, I fell

pregnant with my fourth child. Life with my mother and brother at this point was still quite strained, not just with myself but the children too. Youngsters can sometimes be better judges of character than adults and this certainly was the case. My children kept their grandmother and uncle at arm's length, not really allowing themselves to form close bonds with them. I don't know if this was a result of watching the tension between us or from being inadvertently involved. Of course, it didn't help that they saw me getting upset as the drama unfolded around them and then having to revisit it once we were at home and discussing the visit with my husband. To say that my children had always grown up in and around what went on is an understatement. No matter how much I tried to shield and protect them against it, sometimes they were in the thick of it.

Once when I was six months pregnant, and driving along a coastal road, my mother sat next to me, my brother behind her and in the back with my other three children. At this point, my eldest was seven, my second eldest was five and my third was only coming up a year old. The two eldest children were at the age where they were sponges, listening intently to everything around them. They were also capable of learning from learnt behaviour, regardless of whether this was classed as right or wrong; they would always follow suit from an adult. The older children were more cautious of my brother and didn't really like being in his company. With that being said, my brother was an adult, and you would think he was old enough to lead by example and show children how to respect anyone else. But and believe me it's a big but, he was on the phone to an ex-fiancé at the time and in mid conversation about his own wedding and other such matters, he randomly blurted out, "Oh yeah and by the way, Jessica is still fat!"

Horrified by what I had just heard, I looked at my children in the rear-view mirror, then turned to my mother for support, at the same time as she turned to look out of the window. My children were in the back, need I say more. Nothing and I mean nothing was said, nothing was corrected. Not wanting to cause a scene whilst I was driving and especially with being pregnant, I kept quiet.

Over the years, I had built up the conscious understanding that nothing was to be challenged. Nothing at all. My mother would have denied that she had heard anything until she was blue in the face; saying that I had made it up to cause a scene or argument. So, challenging her would be pointless. A fruitless exercise that would have caused greater harm than good. This is what my life in their company was like. My mother always turning a blind eye to the abuse I suffered.

Desperate to set the record straight as far as my children were concerned, when we got home, I took them to one side and corrected them and enforced in them that it wasn't kind to belittle someone for any reason whether it was justified or not. That if I heard either of them saying things like that to anyone or each other I would not be happy. All of this was said out of earshot from my mother and brother out of fear that they would pick holes or make fun of me for making up tales. My brother was not a child, he is older than me. I was two years of being thirty for

Gods' sake.

I feel now is an appropriate time to bring in some valuable points and that old saying, "People who live in glass houses shouldn't throw stones." During my brother's life as a female, he had a slender physique, he was athletic, not toned but probably just about right. As soon as he started his hormone replacement therapy and the testosterone really took hold, he lost that slender and athletic physique. Instead, it was replaced with a hairy man-beast, who gained weight very quickly. A man with broad shoulders, a big round hairy belly, what's more, he started losing his hair. He had more hair on his round belly and face than he did on his head. My father not only went ash grey at twenty-one years old but he too went bald right on the top of his head. It really was no surprise that my brother would be the same.

So, whilst my brother constantly told me I was fat and ugly right up until I was in my early forties, he himself, was fat, was covered in excess hair and was bald. But here's the bottom line to it all, we, myself or my children, were never and I mean never allowed to make fun of him in any way. We were shot down straight away, but it was okay for my mother to listen to him ripping into me and saying things that weren't even true.

After years of struggling with hair loss and fast forwarding to 2021, my brother eventually resorted to wearing a hairpiece; not just any hairpiece, but one that was glued in place.

Then one unassuming day, my mother secretly

pulled me to one side, she felt she couldn't contain the news any longer, she told me the unspeakable had happened. During a night of passion with his girlfriend and lacking the confidence to tell her he wore a hairpiece and that he was in fact bald underneath, he became hairless for one night only. Somehow, at the height of passion, his hairpiece became stuck to her bed's headboard and ripped off, leaving him feeling rather more naked than he had hoped. Need I say more, I thought I was going to die from laughing so hard.

But despite my mother coming to me and volunteering this information freely, she would only laugh at my brother out of his ear- and eye-shot. She would have her moment and then compose herself. Never mentioning it again. Whenever anyone would raise it with him present, she would shout and scowl. He would walk off about to burst into tears, slamming and shouting and she would go running after him, trying to soothe and pander to him.

He had told her in confidence and she had told me, she knew she had told me and broken his confidence and he knew she had told me. How else would I have found out. It was such a vicious circle, a tightly woven web of denial, deceit and mistrust, as well as a cycle of emotional abuse, I didn't know whether I was coming or going with my mother. It was like she enjoyed luring me in on a thin fishing line and then letting the reel out. I never knew where I stood with her.

I digress too much …

CHAPTER 8: TAKING BACK CONTROL...

After losing my grandfather, I felt I had nothing keeping me in my home county. A move to Norfolk saw the distance between the three of us grow wider and was very much welcomed from my side. I could start living a life without either of them shadowing me or judging my ever movement.

My mother was already an absent grandmother and had been from the start, despite living walking distance from us. When she did have the children for me, she made me feel as if I had to be eternally grateful. Who else has to give their parents pocket money for their children when they spend time with grandparents? My mother constantly said how much they cost her and how she couldn't afford it, if she took them out for the day, I had to give her the money for them. Guilt tripping me was my mother's favourite pastime, even when we went to stay with her for longer than 5 days, she divided the water, gas and electric bill for that time period between myself, my children and her, not to mention I had to do a full weeks shop costing over £100 for the time we were there. As you can probably imagine, our visits got fewer and fewer. Don't get me wrong, I have never considered, 'Going home' a free hide, but she never once offered when she came to stay with us, she never once put her hand in her pocket to help us out. My brother was even worse as an uncle, they would be lucky if they saw him once a year. He wouldn't make any time for the children at all.

My eldest son has just one photo of the two of them together. The other children have no photographs of them, or any good memories of time spent together. The only memories they hold are of him having a go at me, poking fun at me, telling me I was fat in front of them, treating me like general crap and not surprisingly, shouting at my mother when she did something wrong or went against what he wanted or said.

Fast forward to 2012 with a little update in between.

By 2009 I was on my own with four children. I'd had a daughter in 2007 and had coped with my own relationship breakdown for many years prior and it seemed like the natural way forward. I had decided to remain in Norfolk, as this was where I had made a life for myself and with the children. I hadn't got anything to go back to my home county for, so why not.

I ended up working three jobs, one as a makeup artist doing weddings and proms, one working at an equine yard, and one setting up my own equine business whilst retraining and studying for an equine yard manager's course. I managed to complete a two-year course in just six months with top marks. Additionally, I was funding the two older children in private school, which wasn't a boarding school, all whilst keeping my head above water. All on my own, I will add! No support from anyone else. I even helped to buy a new washing machine and tumble dryer for my mother because she said she was struggling financially. Looks like I was a bit of a Muppet for thinking and believing it. Just like anyone who is trapped within an abusive relationship, the promise of better times and hope that things will change, is one of the foremost reasons why a cycle of abuse can't be changed until you are ready to change it.

She only ever helped me out during the course of my adulthood to the tune of £10,000 and this was over the course of ten years. Despite this, she had helped my brother out with sums in excess of £500,000 over the same period. She even helped him buy a £750,000 home in 2021, which she funded half of and then proceeded to tell me she had left her half of her estate to him in her will. I was a single mother raising four children and working three jobs. All he did at that time was gamble and rack up debts. Seems ironic really.

My brother had arranged that he and my mother would come to me for the Easter weekend of 2012. It wasn't my first choice by any means, and I couldn't back out, he pressurised me into it. My mother had arrived ahead of my brother and his new wife. This was a different wife from the phone call in the car and also from the one with the unfortunate sticky hairpiece situation.

For weeks prior to their arrival, I had gone into a state of panic, with the children wondering what the hell I was doing. I frantically cleaned the house and told the children they had no idea what my brother was like. They had gone six years without seeing him and had all but forgotten what he was like. My dealings with my brother were well and truly ingrained in my soul.

One of the days before my brother's arrival, driving home from having taken the day off from studying and work to take my mother shopping, she turned to me and said, "You have to take your hat off to him; after everything he's been through, you must be proud of him." I paused for a moment, whilst continuing to drive and in slight disbelief, patiently waiting for her to realise what she had just said out aloud and waiting for her to recognise my own achievements and efforts and for her to say how proud she was of me, which never came. No matter what I did in my life, I could never amount to what my brother did nor could or would I ever get the chance to step up on his golden pedestal or my own for that matter. My mother never saw me than anything other than an emotional battering ram, an annoyance that constantly got in the way.

I'm sorry what? Was the only thought going through my head at the time. I must be proud of him?! Hmmm, what about me? Did I not come into the same statement or thought process?

Whilst I do agree with the statement and to a certain degree, yes. What he has gone through has been an achievement, but why should I be proud of him? He's not proud of me. It hasn't made him a better person. It hasn't changed how he is with me or anyone else. He had spent a lifetime bullying me and tormenting me; why should I be proud of that? And what about me? What about my achievements? He may have overcome a physical barrier and managed to change that but it never changed his outlook on anything else, he still looked down on anyone else around him. He still treated me and anyone else like dirt, including his own mother. How is that something to be proud of?

My mother once said to me, that her sole purpose in this lifetime was to be here for her son. To make sure he was cared for and had everything he needed to live his life. No mention of me. There was no recognition on her face of what she had just said out loud. There was no, "Oh, I didn't quite mean it like that."

I am just a by-product; an afterthought. I know that my mother never once saw me in the same light as she saw him. I have spent my entire life in the shadow of my brother. Whatever I did, I would never equal him. I would always stand in the shadow of his shining light.

Eventually, D-Day arrived; the moment I had been dreading.

His arrival with his ageing alcoholic, non-maternal wife, came with the most daunting dark cloud that overshadowed the house for the entire weekend. The very first thing he did after stepping over the threshold was to run his finger along any and every surface, checking for dust. My children stood there in disbelief. My mother behaved as if this were the norm, trying to laugh it off. And sure enough, I didn't get any praise or recognition for anything.

I remember turning to my eldest and whispering to him, "Now you know why I cleaned the house from top to bottom."

Despite the frantic cleaning, he still found a small amount of dust and showed his displeasure at how dirty my house was by tutting aloud. Turning to my mother and his wife, pointing his outstretched finger at them and waggling it in their faces and showing his distain that I was failing in my duty as a mother. Not once referring to what I was doing or how the children were. It was just my failings and by his standards only. I was not failing; I was in my element and I knew it and held on to it.

Everyone was on edge, from that moment on. The atmosphere in the house was awful. You could have cut it with a knife.

This was the last time I spent with my mother and brother. I finally had the courage to stand up to him for shouting at my children in their own home and for laughing at something so silly, only the boys know what it was. We were having Sunday dinner in silence when the boys started to giggle at something. A giggle turned into laughter, which despite their best efforts got louder and louder. I could see my brother's face getting redder and redder and I asked the boys to quieten down. They did, but by this point they had got the giggles badly.

I caught my mother glancing at my brother and she asked them to stop. They didn't and I didn't step in. My thought was, they were in their own home, they weren't doing anything wrong. They didn't have enough of a relationship with their uncle to make them want to listen to him. Well, that was our fate sealed.

My brother screamed at the boys to stop and then

proceeded to smash his fists hard enough against the kitchen table, that everything flew in to the air. The boys stopped and gulped. I turned to my mother and slowly rose from the table and went over to the kitchen sink. She followed and asked if there was anything she could do. I turned to her, smiled and said, "Yes, you can all foxtrot oscar out of my house!"

Sure enough, they didn't waste any time in getting up and packing their bags. They didn't even bring their dirty plates from the table to the sink.

Standing up to my brother came at a cost. By doing so, my mother went running with her tail between her legs after him and all the way home. She didn't try to mediate the situation, she never asked how I felt or how the children felt. She couldn't see it from my point of view, that he didn't have the right to chastise my children in their own home for something so minor. She was out the door and sitting in the car quicker than I could finish the washing up. It was abundantly clear where I stood in my family.

It cemented my relationship with the both of them. In all honesty, we weren't going to miss them. You can't miss something you never had and unfortunately the children never had a grandmother's or uncle's presence in their lives anyway. So, what did it matter.

There's no doubting that my brother fitted into his new body. He had spent a lifetime honing his attitude and how he thought a male should act that now his physically appearance matched his attitude, it almost gave him the permission to act manly and with authority even when he was not entitled to it. It gave him what he needed to behave with the bullying attitude and to think he could get away with it because my mother never stood up to him, he hated anyone who challenged him. I had grown up with it, I was very much accustomed to it, but my children weren't. And I wasn't about to have them caught up in it.

The full transition was the right way for him. Yes, he wore a scar on his forearm, from the reconstructive surgery. Yes, he wore the scars of the double mastectomy underneath his hairy chest. No, it didn't actually make him a better person. It hadn't changed his outlook at all. He hadn't been humbled by his experience and he hadn't learnt that after all those years of mental health issues, that others may be suffering too.

My brother refused to acknowledge any element of suffering that I had endured and sustained.

From that moment right up to August 2018, I had no contact with either of them. In all honesty, this was a huge relief. One of the biggest I have ever experienced.

I hadn't quite appreciated the pressure I had felt from all angles in trying to cope with how they made me feel. With what they put me through. I wasn't fighting for my mother's attention or acknowledgment anymore for anything I did. And I wasn't looking for that seal of approval. I could live and do what I wanted without the fear of being judged or put down or feeling the need to justify myself to them. No more was I having to fight against someone who was so negative. I physically felt a huge weight lift from my shoulders.

Being a single parent with four children was not the easiest. But I was going to do the best I could.

CHAPTER 9: LIFE IS A DILEMMA …

When I sat down to write this book, my intention were pure. I wanted these pages to help just one other person in dealing with transgender – transitioning – LGBTQ+ - the mental health issues, all manner of things surroundings these areas and the hope that someone out there who has felt lost in needing help 'coming out' to friends and family, who may identify with elements this book, to know that your aren't the failure, you aren't the fault or broken in any which way. That if someone has an issue with you, then the issue is theirs and theirs alone. These issues come with a complex, tightly woven web of interlinking thoughts, feelings, emotions and processes, it's not straight forward and there is no easy answer or way round it. Even I had appreciated or anticipated just how complex it could all get.

I have found that after completion, I am having to rewrite this later section of the book. Which in hindsight and after going through a plethora of emotions, I am seeing the silver lining and the positives that could come from the rewriting.

What I will say is, that Part Two contains even more complexity, with twists and turns and unexpected stories. They are all real, I can assure you for that. And despite the fact that some sections have had additions or subtractions in their content, there are lots of stories that merge and cross paths, with some stories needing to be told, to aid change and help those seeking help. It may get confusing at times but they all deserve a place amongst the lines on these pages.

As I have already mentioned, I have lived with double standards and contradictions all my life not to mention having it drummed in to me that I am worthless and unlovable. I had been conditioned into believing I didn't have a place in this world or that no one would ever listen to me or take me seriously. But I have learnt that I do have a worth and value in this life and I do have a right to have my voice heard, whether people like it or not.

It has been tiring to be constantly looking over your shoulder and judged and put down. And yes, at times this has involved my own children judging me and digging holes in things that I have done. I have never proclaimed to be perfect, but for those in my family that have, they have been the furthest from perfect. The impressionable years watching my brother and mother, set the seeds for some underlying behavioral traits which I have absorbed and have learnt to accept from others, and despite my best efforts, I have not been able to reverse all of them. However, I have been very careful not to carry them forward into my own children. Respect has always been a big issue within our family. We have lacked it on a large scale. My mother and brother never once shown me an ounce of respect, and yes, while I could take the upper hand and not stoop as low as them, I am a firm believer in 'Treat others just as you want to be treated', Luke 6:31-36.

The requests that I have mentioned, which are placed on family and friends, dealing with transitioning, can sometimes be the hardest part of the process to deal with. I watched as my brother forced my mother to remove any and all photographic evidence of before and requested that she destroy it. I have be forced myself to deny all knowledge that I have ever had a sister, which, for me, was a double edge sword. While I was happy to live in the acknowledgement of not having a sister any more, I also had to cope with the consequences of our past, with joint old school friends and friends of the family. Despite the demand, I wasn't given any alternative explanation to use, so when I was backed into a corner by an old school friend, I had to think on the hoof. All I could muster was that my sister had died. As a young person, who had not had the support from the get go, I really don't see that I had any other option. To a certain degree, yes, effectively, she had. My sister no longer existed. But, when I was hounded by my brother as to what I had said, regardless of trying to always do the right thing, I got it wrong. I was shouted at, I was called all the names under the sun and once that all settled, I just stood there and said, "What would you of liked me to say?". My brother's reply was, "Well, anything other than that!" "Then you should of given me what you wanted me to say," came my reply, and I walked off, knowing that he couldn't answer his own question. However, I find that he has totally contracted himself. I know for a fact that he had confided in an old school friend that he had transitioned, which didn't go to plan. The thought of returning to our old school had never been on the cards for him because he would knowingly be putting himself in the very situation he had spent over twenty years avoiding. Until recently. Our old school offered their five yearly Alumni Reunion and to my surprise I saw my brother's name on the list of attendees. At some point he would have had to explain to the school staff who he was and who he is now. So therefore he has broken the very first demand he placed on us and become a hypocrite, by knowingly entering a place of history as one person and knowingly knowing he would have to explain that should anyone ask who he was. It just so happened that he kept himself to himself the entire time and didn't partake in talking with anyone. Some would seriously argue what was the point of wasting four hours of his day. And some would argue that it was his choice to put himself in the position so that makes it all ok. He would be in control of the situation, which clearly he wouldn't be.

Alongside the demand for erasing history, I have been asked to live a life of secrets and lies, which while I totally understand why and have shown respect throughout, especially when it has not been deserved, I am aiding and abetting the deception. At times I have found it unbearable to cope with.

It is one thing to lie about something someone may or may not have done in life to feel accepted, but to knowingly lie about something that affects a whole family in order to gain acceptance, in my view is wrong. You can't ask nor expect someone to carry a lie and go about their daily business. It doesn't work like that. Equally, I also know that shouting it from the roof tops is just as unacceptable. Unless anyone transitioning moves to a different country there will always be times when events crop up which are unexpected and challenging. There needs to be great deal of communication around the subject and how it will be broached.

Some or all of the points I have raised here, will be explained at the right time further into each chapter. If I were to lace them here, they would be more confusing and taken out of context.

But what I will say, is that both sides of whatever is going on, needs to acknowledge each other and allow a safe time and place to have their side listened too and validated.

There is no right or wrong, but it is wrong to not appreciate how someone else is feeling. You may not understand it and know how to deal with it and you may think it's absurd and so far from the truth, but you need to allow that time for discussion.

We are all involved in everyone's lives, let's learn to be accepting and responsible people.

PART TWO
A MIXED TRANSITION…

CHAPTER 10
GOING BACK TO MOTHERHOOD...

When my first second child was eighteen months old, he ended up having extreme eczema all over his body and head. Bath time was painful and laborious which saw our nightly routine consist of creaming and wet wrapping which sometimes was very hard for us both to cope with. His head suffered the worst. Massive clumps of skin joined together, stopping new hair growth from getting through and leaving noticeable bald patches.

It took nearly a year of hard work and patience to deal with it but his fighting spirit never gave up in battling through the pain. Our hard work eventually paid off and throughout the subsequent years he had a head of hair you would have died for or paid through the nose for at a salon. Hair that reached all the way down her back with naturally blonde highlights in all the right places.

From the age of two, my second child knew his own mind. I appreciate that not all mothers want daughters and not all fathers want sons. But, after having a boy first, I became over excited at the range of girl's clothes on the market. I had spent the first two years dressing him in pretty girly clothes, dresses, skirts, matching outfits, in all the colours associated with girls. But those times soon went. Everything I expected a girl to do, he rejected and that was fine. It was never enforced or imposed at any point. It didn't make him happy, so why attempt to put him through doing it just to make me happy. As he started growing into his own person and knowing his own mind, he felt more comfortable and at home in trousers, jeans or shorts.

I would like to think that my daughter had a happy childhood. Parenting isn't easy and at no point have I ever sat here and said, I got it right. In fact, like all other parents who are open minded and open to their screwups, I got it wrong more often than not. But I always tried my best and I always put the children above my needs. He was able to do what he wanted, he was never forced to do or not do anything.

Even back when he was six years old plus, he was at ease playing football. There wasn't a girls' team, and even if there had been, I don't think he would have wanted to play in it. he played for a mixed football team and was a valued member.

Stood on the side-lines of the pitch, I started noticing how differently girls were treated from boys and the challenges facing the lesser sex. That's when I started really challenging the hurdles. I saw the disappointment on my daughter's face and I wasn't going to stand for it. And why not; parents should be about raising equal opportunity and awareness of female and male capabilities and what makes each gender comfortable in their own skin. I felt it was my role and duty to fight for my child. The suffragettes would have been proud to have us fighting their corner. Not just fighting for female rights but fighting for any gender to be able to do anything without fear of stigma or ridicule.

As a mother, my main priority was to allow my children to express themselves and to be who they wanted to be. I had spent a lifetime conforming to what my parents expected and wanted my brother and I to be and I wasn't going to impose that on my own children.

Over the years, my second child fitted in better being surrounded by boys. He was accepted and comfortable and I had no issues with that. I also fitted in better with boys when I was growing up. I didn't trust girls, probably because of what my sister had done to me. Amongst the boys I felt I wasn't judged or put down. My second child felt the same.

Previously, I had mentioned that I was able to send the two eldest children to private secondary school. Arron thrived but my second child hated it. He struggled being around, in his words, "Pretentious, beautified girls, living off Daddy's money" who insisted on acting and looking the same as the girl next door. As he would put it, he wanted to go back to a normal state school and be surrounded by normal people living a normal life. I had raised a strong individual forward-thinking girl, who had his own mind and didn't want to conform to what was expected of the female race and I was proud of that.

At the age of eleven, I gently nudged him to join the Sea Cadets. He was afraid of water and quite frankly I needed a break from attending three lots of football training and matches a week.

It wasn't surprising that he excelled. Within the first six months he had managed to gain the Commodores Pennant. In all the seventy years of that unit being open, only one other person had gained it. He was the first female. I have never been so proud. What an achievement. I do hope that he never ever forgets where he came from and what he managed to achieve throughout his life. Regardless of the future, achievements are still achievements and those cannot be taken away from that person, whoever they end up being.

We fast forward to 2014, by this point I had been a single mother for just over five years, which saw us move down to another county and lots of other changes, like the breakdown of my relationship with Arron and the secret talks he was having with his grandmother, a new relationship for me, which resulted in me getting remarried in 2015. The move resulted in a change of school for all the children but most of all for my second child, which was a welcome relief. He was surrounded with people that he could understand and get on with, without having to pretend.

Sitting on the side lines and watching him evolve, it was evident that things were changing. He was starting to accept that he was different and worked hard to understand why. Finally, he was starting to fit in.

I do feel that Generation Z (millennial babies) and beyond are so lucky to be in such a unique position. The circles he was moving in were so accepting and he wasn't on his own. He had friends who were going through similar emotions, which meant that he had someone to talk to. To iron out things and get them right in his own head.

One day in 2017, he came home and said he had a girlfriend; it was a day like any other. In all honesty, it never bothered me in the slightest; my now ex-husband just laughed and said, "Okay." The younger children accepted it, but I think it was this point that sealed his and Arron's relationship. For whatever reasons, he could never accept it. Life with him in the house became unbearable. You could have cut the atmosphere with a knife 24/7, that was until he moved out. Other than that, my second child's relationship was never brought to the table for discussion or comment. I could see how happy it made him and that's all I cared about.

You know when spring comes and new life starts growing and budding, over time you watch this bud grow from being tiny and green, wondering what it will be, to see it forming in to a beautiful flower just before blossoming. This is the only way I can describe how I felt watching my children's lives unfold.

I think this set the tone for everything else to come. Not just with him but for the other children too. They could see that I encouraged; I didn't judge. These were the foundations to everything else to come; not just for him but for his sister too.

Children don't ask to be born. None of us are asked beforehand, yet we are all expected to conform to unwritten stereotypes. We are all individuals and should be treated as such. We all have our own paths and directions but more importantly we all have our own things that make us happy. So what, if the person next door to us doesn't like what makes us happy. At the end of the day, once that person is behind their own four walls, what the hell does it matter? How does it affect them? It's nobody else's business what makes us happy. We have one life, and we should be able to live that life in the best way possible. Free from ridicule and judgement from others.

CHAPTER 11: **THERES NO GOING BACK...**

Between 2014 to 2018 I had coped with a massive roller coaster of mental health challenges brought on by my soon to be ex-husband and my eldest son. Even though I wasn't talking with my mother, she contributed to it as well. She had a huge and detrimental effect on Arron, drip feeding him poison about me, slating me as a mother, telling him I didn't love him or want him and that I should have put him first. How I had let him down. She drummed it into him that he could leave our home at the age of sixteen and move in with her, where she would look after him and provide for him correctly.

Slowly but surely his attitude towards me and everyone and everything changed. He became aggressive, argumentative, challenging and bigoted towards everyone. We trod on eggshells around him which made life very difficult and unpleasant. I also had to deal with a life-threatening pregnancy that rocked me to my very core as well as the start of two long-term health conditions which didn't present themselves fully until 2021. Through everything, my second child was by my side. He was my rock. No one saw my dark side more. At the time and even now, I am incredibly grateful for the support I received from him. He never judged. Never said, 'I told you so', or made me feel any worse than I felt.

However, putting that to one side, 2018 was to be the start of an amazing journey for him.

It all started in March 2018. After years of battling the medical profession, I was finally preparing for life threatening surgery. I won't lie and pretend that I wasn't scared. All I was thinking about was making it through the day to see my children. What happened next gave me the inspiration and drive to cope with it.

On the morning of my surgery, whilst I was sorting out my bag for hospital, I came across a letter addressed to me. It was handwritten, in familiar writing. I sat down to read it, thinking that the children had written a note to say how scared they were too, but that everything would be fine. I couldn't have been more wrong.

I sat in the kitchen, alone and read it. Tears streaming down my face. I would love to share everything that was in the letter. And, although I was asked to bin the letter some time afterwards, I can't add in any more than what is below. As a parent, we like to retain special moments for when we get old and forgetful, therefore we never really throw anything away. Just for the record and although I have told a porky to my second child, I did in fact keep the letter. The letter was addressed to me, so in theory it is for me to do with what I like. It remains safe in a box that no one knows exists. It's my box and mine alone.

Letter to Mum:

"I don't want you to die and not know the truth about me. All my life I have tried fitting in but never ..."

I already knew what was coming. I didn't need to read anymore. I had spent the last seventeen years waiting for this moment.

I reached for my laptop, opened it and started penning my reply …

"My darling daughter,

From the minute you were born, I have loved you unconditionally and will always love you unconditionally. I am so grateful for the life I have been given. Although sometimes I have struggled with how hard my life has been, I have come such a long way personally and spiritually. From being a very closed book to being so open and accepting of any situation life wants to throw at me.

I have always known what was going to be the outcome in your life and I have had many years to prepare myself and you for the new journey and chapter that we will go through together. I will be with you every step of the way and I will give you as much love, support and guidance as you want. If it's fine by you then it's fine by me.

We have such a special relationship; one that I cherish massively. In fact, I don't know how I would cope without you here, so on that basis I will keep you locked up and at home with me!

I am so very very proud of who you are and what you've achieved in your life. We haven't had it easy and yes, certain people haven't made it easy. And, if it means people not accepting, then they are not worth being in either of our lives. You are worth more to me than a pretend son. You have been there every step of the way for me, and I will be there every step of the way for you.

Mary Kay said, "There is only one way to eat an elephant: a bite at a time.". It's going to be a slow process and at times hard, but we can do it together. The end result will be worth the wait!

I wish I hadn't wasted Grampy's name on your older brother, he's not worthy of it. Grampy was everything that you are, beautiful, strong, kind, tolerant, caring, loving and so very cheeky.

I love you with all my heart, there is no reason to feel alone or upset. We can conquer anything.

Always and forever,

Your loving Mum, xx"

I emailed him straight away and before I left for the hospital. I was desperate for him to know that I had received his letter and that everything would be okay, so he didn't worry throughout the day.

At the time, I didn't even mention anything to my soon to be ex-husband. I wasn't sure how he would take the news. With a selfish head on, he wasn't his father and I didn't really care what he thought. My time with him was fast coming to an end.

Whilst I sat alone, waiting for my operation, I thought about booking him in to the hairdressers. Hair for anyone is so important; it would be the foundation and starting block of his journey. We had worked so hard over the last thirteen years to rectify his hair issues caused by the eczema. I didn't want his hair to go to waste, so I searched for and found the Little Princess Trust and thought this would be something he would want to do too.

Deep down, I did know one thing and I knew I had the balls to say it, despite everything that had happened. I also knew I wasn't going to like it, but it could be the best thing for him. There was only one person better than myself to help him and guide him, and that was my brother. Having been through the whole process from start to finish, he knew everything that my child would need to know. So, I told him he had to reach out to his uncle. Although he hadn't been there for him for so many years, I thought he would be the best person to have on his side.

Unfortunately, I would be proved very wrong much later on in 2020/1, he wasn't the right person to have turned to. In hindsight I probably knew what was coming, but I wanted my child to feel he had the support from everyone. That he wasn't going down this road on his own.

The main goal now was to focus on a new start. September would see the start of a new college life, a new place, new faces and a new start away from everyone that had known him before.

That night when I came home from hospital, was the last night I had with him and the first morning with my son, Jack. New beginnings awaited him. I sat and watched the sense of relief lift from his shoulders. He was finally finding his own way to become happy.

That happiness did come at a cost though. Jack placed one demand on me that looking back, I should have said more about at the time.

Having spoken to many others in the same situation, it would appear that this request is quite a common one. However, I feel it is hard to expect anyone to adhere to it.

He asked that I remove all and every trace of his past, anything that referred to him as her, meaning that every letter, card, every photo or gift with his name on it, basically everything that was before and no longer part of his future. Not only that, he was asking and expecting me to remove my and his siblings past because all the photos prior to the transition were of him as a female.

Having a request like that placed or even thrust upon you is can seem unfair and sometimes hurtful. Regardless of how the person transitioning feels, as parents and as siblings, we have feelings too. Although it could be argued that the transitionee and their siblings have an easier time adjusting to demands like this; nevertheless they are being asked to effectively erase themselves from history, which is not fair. I do understand that out of respect for the transitionee, removing past items is respecting their wishes but it is apart of history that involves many people, non the less.

Whilst I agree that the main focus should be and is on the person going through the transition, there has to be an element of focus on us as parents/siblings and friends too.

I have every right to keep those cards, letters, gifts and photos. They are mine to keep. My history, my memories and part of my future. That doesn't mean to say that I would exploit them or show them to anyone who would look at them or ask to see them. They are there to serve my memory and to remind me of my family's moments in history.

A human being should not place requests on another to destroy their past. I treasure those memories and by asking me to remove them, I am being denied those moments. I am also being offered nothing in replacement because there is nothing to replace them with. It's not possible to magically rewrite history and provide me or anyone else including the transitionee with fresh new pictures just the way you want them to be. And while we may feel hurt and upset at that, equally for the transitionee, it must be incredibly difficult to deal with.

I am incredibly proud of Jack's journey, and I will continue to remain proud, but I should also be allowed to remember how it all started.

So, I have a box with all the photos, letters, cards etc that were given to me by him. It is my box and for my viewing only. It is my history, my journey alongside him and my other children. They are there for when I am too old and frail to rely on my memory bank. They are mine and they are to stay. It's not up for negotiation.

CHAPTER 12: AND SO, THE JOURNEY BEGINS...

We identify the season of Spring with the start of new beginnings, sowing the seeds for new growth to come in the summer months. Late summer of 2018 was the start of the new beginning for Jack. One he had hoped for, for such a long time. Just as I suggested, he had reached out to his uncle for support and advice. I wasn't a part of that and I had no need for him to be in my own life. But I knew he needed to be there for my son and that was enough.

With his new name chosen and the official paperwork sent off, a new hair style and a new wardrobe, things were moving in the right direction.

I remember his first haircut. After long talks with the hairdresser, he sat in the chair beaming from ear to ear. This was it, the defining moment and his new start.

As the hairdresser sectioned out his hair into the requirements from the Little Princess Trust, a slight pang of sadness passed over me. We had spent years working so hard to get him a perfect head of hair and now it was all going. What helped the process – for me especially – was the look on his face and the fact that wigs were going to be made for children going through cancer. Could there have been a better way of starting this process?

When the hairdresser had finished, we all stood there saying nothing. I think we had all held our breath, which, being an emotional person at the best of times, kick started me off. Tears of happiness I will add. Don't panic it wasn't a sign of regret.

From the moment we stepped out of the hairdressers, his confidence just came from nowhere. It was amazing. Just a simple change in appearance and his whole world was starting to change. I knew then that we were on the right path.

Clothes shopping was next and to be honest there wasn't that much of a change from what he had been wearing anyway.

Next on the list of our hurdles was talking to his siblings and sorting out schooling, both before and after.

Telling the other children didn't faze me at all. But I think this worried him to a degree. I don't know why because we had always been so open. Able to discuss anything in front of any of them. I guess one can never truly gauge how someone will take certain news or process change etc. I don't remember the order in which I told his siblings, but I do remember who reacted and how.

Shaun was thirteen, right on the cusp of adolescence, things could of gone either way. In fact, he was brilliant; he didn't have any questions or concerns. I think the only thing going through his mind was, he had an extra brother to spa with, brilliant!

Emily was eleven at the time and was just amazing. She

didn't bat an eyelid and just accepted the new change. She also had a strong bond with Jack and knew deep down that it was the right path for him. Other than lots of questions which we did our best to answer, that was that.

My youngest son, Fred was three. He had a very close relationship with Jack and still does. However, there is only so much you can say or explain to a three-year-old because they can't process things in the same way an older person can. Having said that, we explained everything in simple terms so that he could understand enough, and again, that was it. No more was said. All he cared about was that his closest sibling was still his closest sibling. He still looked the same, he still smelt the same and he still gave him hugs and kisses in the same way. Nothing had changed as far as he was concerned, other than his name and the fact he didn't have the long hair he could wipe his sticky fingers on; or play with it until it got tangled. All of which took a day to get used to.

Telling his eldest brother, Arron, however was harder than I had ever thought. There was a two-year age gap and the conversation didn't go the way I thought or hoped it would. As you may have guessed, I have a no fuss approach to everything and I have never sugar coated anything that needed telling to the children. I have often come up against a lot of people disagreeing with me on my approach but my argument is that they have grown up to be well balanced and able to process difficult situations with ease. I'd like to think that I take everything in my stride and I hope that that approach rubs off on the children.

Sadly, this approach didn't go to plan with Arron. He didn't want to know. He refused to accept the news or to change towards him, which came as a massive blow to me and to Jack Particularly considering that he had grown up knowing about his uncle and had no issues in dealing with that. His reaction would set the foundations for what happened further down the line. My mother had continued her campaign of hate towards me and intensified her poison drip by drip. Not literally, just in metaphoric terms.

Moving on from that blow and during the summer of 2018 Jack started preparing for his prom. It was very exciting for all of us as Arron hadn't wanted to go to his. There was much excitement as this would be the first prom for the family. After much deliberation, Jack finally settled on an aubergine/ burgundy coloured three-piece suit, which suited him so well. On the night, he was flanked by two of his closest girlfriends from school, myself, Emily and Fred. It was also the first time since leaving school, that he would be meeting up with friends that didn't know about his transition. They would be seeing a whole new person, presenting himself with new hair, a new name and a new wardrobe. Despite his underlying nerves, the night went well and everyone accepted him and the others going through the same, for who they were.

Now when a boy goes to a party in a ball gown, no one really bats an eyelid and why not. The only thing I'm jealous of is how much better they are at pulling off wearing a beautiful dress and walking in high heels than I am!

Putting his eldest brother to one side and not letting it affect the progress we were making, we moved on to dealing with the schooling issues.

We had two schools to deal with. Jack's school whilst he was taking his GCSEs and the college he would be going on to.

Not everyone or everywhere was as advanced as we were. This just highlighted how backwards we as humans were in our way of dealing with *difficult* issues.

You might think that back in 2018, which in terms of history isn't that long ago, with life changing constantly and the politically correct drum banging in the background, that the need to teach acceptance should have been a high priority. Those in whom we entrust our children would be the first to iron out anything and everything and wave the inclusivity/diversity banner in people's faces. But it didn't quite work like that. They can more often than not be the ones who hinder the process. Many through ignorance and lack of education in understanding and many through bringing their own beliefs to the table and not allowing anyone else to acknowledge their existence the way they need to.

Having passed his GCSEs, the time came to find a college for his A levels. Jack had already made his decision for obvious reasons, he wasn't staying on for sixth form at his previous school, he wanted to make a fresh start.

We phoned the college of his choice in late July, early August and arranged a one-to-one meeting with the head of college, ahead of the new term starting in September. I had made the process we were going through clear on the phone and she assured me everything would be in hand. We were desperate for the new college to be open to all things relating to diversity. It didn't happen.

As we were walking through the college, I remember thinking to myself the head of college was just stumbling around for answers and really didn't have a clue about what she was doing or saying.

This suggested that she hadn't prepared for the meeting by doing any research or fully understanding the requirements needed in a situation like ours. Nothing was planned out for anyone remotely in Jack's position, no contingency plans had been put in place. It was as if he was speaking double Dutch to her. Watching his face as he took the lead; asking questions about how they would cope? What would they do? Where would he get changed? And realising that his new fresh start was going to end up being even more restrictive and segregated than before.

Going from seeing him being so excited to then feeling so crushed was soul destroying for both of us. I remember sitting in the head's office, gob smacked and stunned into silence at what we were dealing with. With Jack begging me not to make a big deal out of it.

The college was not gender fluid. They weren't even remotely prepared. He was shown a grubby, tiny, dirty hole to change in for PE lessons. And, because treatment hadn't officially started and wouldn't until he turned eighteen, if he was lucky, he was still going to be made to use the female toilets. Talk about adding insult to injury. There was nothing gender neutral about the college. All I could muster was, "Are you sure you want to go here?"

After much discussion and reassurance from the Head, which didn't help convince us anymore, Jack decided to go ahead and enroll. After all, there wasn't much choice in the matter. All the other colleges were over thirty minutes away from home and as he was needing to rely on public transport it wasn't going to be viable.

With one school down, we had the other school to address.

The summer came and went and he was fitting into his new way of life. He had an amazing circle of friends, (and still has the same amazing circle of friends) surrounding him and supporting him. One of his friendship group was going through the same process, male to female. Sadly, they weren't able to go to the same college but in the evenings and on weekends they made time to get together.

With the end of the summer holidays fast approaching, there was great anticipation for the GCSE presentation, which would see Jack's whole year group getting together for one final night at the school.

I was going without my ex-husband; I quite often did a lot of everything with just myself and the children. I didn't mind at all to be honest, the less time I had to spend with my ex-husband the better.

I had chosen to sit at the back of the hall with Fred who

was still at that playful mischievous stage; just in front of me and to the side, were a whole row of teachers.

The moment came when Jack's name was called. He had spoken with the people organising the presentation and told them over and over about his name change. The last thing he wanted was to deal with embarrassment on the night. His name was called and on to the stage he went.

We stood and clapped and Fred blurted out his name as loud as he could and waved. Instead of it being one of my proudest moments, I found my attention was taken from my son and had crashed down beside me to focus on what was being said next to me. In the same row as mine and six seats to my left, two rows of teachers were sat. They were discussing the students as they came on to the stage. All I could hear was whispering between them, they were racking their brains to work out who Jack was.

"Who's that? I don't remember anyone called that?"

"Oh, yeah that's … now known as …"

In that moment, I sank back into my seat, my heart pounding and feeling as if all I wanted to do was to shout at them and tell them how ignorant and unprofessional they were. But I didn't. I didn't want Fred to see an argument and I didn't want to make a scene for Jack on the stage. This moment was for Jack and I wasn't going to spoil it. It was clear that the school had suffered from a lack of communication on a grave scale.

The only thing I could do was to phone the school the next morning. My natural instinct was to rip their throats out but I settled for making them feel worthless and small.

Having spoken with Jack and having told him, his reaction was to do nothing. I felt it was my duty as a mother and as a mother of a transitioning child to raise this point with them so that it stopped them making someone else feel like crap.

How dare they do that and in public. I criticised the headmaster for his poor handling of staff management and his lack of being able to uphold the staff professionally whilst at school. I asked him if he thought he could be proud of those staff members on that day and how he and those staff members had let the school as a whole down. I vowed from that point on, that no one was going to make me, or my family feel like that again.

I totally understand that everyone is fully entitled to have their own opinion, we all do, and I totally understand that everyone has the freedom of speech. However, people in a profession that is surrounded by other impressionable people need to remember to leave their freedom of speech at home. They should remain thoughtful, professional and dignified at all times, whilst keeping their thoughts well and truly inside their own heads. Learnt behaviour is one of the hardest qualities to change or lose. No one should impose their own thoughts or beliefs on anyone else. No one should have that right. No one has the right to belittle anyone for their beliefs or disbeliefs; no matter who it is. If they do, then they need to have a long hard look at themselves and work out what they are missing in their own lives in order to feel the need to make someone else feel unworthy.

Sadly, school wasn't the only time when we came against bigots or uneducated people.

My own mother has harbored and encouraged a bigot within the family, which is inconceivable when you think she is a mother of a transgender child too.

It is with a heavy heart and words that I thought I would never say, my mother encouraged her own grandchild, my eldest son, Arron to be a bigot. You could then argue that my own mother could be considered as one for encouraging this. It is not the first time that we have dealt with other bigots within our family. My unfortunate husbands and their families are too.

CHAPTER 13: PEOPLE WHO LIVE IN GLASS HOUSES SHOULDN'T THROW STONES ...

Not that I wish to mention anything about my second ex-husband, but I feel at this point he actually has some relevance for many different reasons. Not just because of him but his family too and to prove that being a bigot can be an inbred issue and how the importance of learnt behaviour within a family setting really does have an effect. I hope it also highlights that people's exterior sometimes doesn't match their interior. You can never truly know what people are thinking or feeling; the best you can hope for is that you don't judge them or hate them for how they perceive themselves, even if they don't give back the same. In most cases, which generation people come from can also have a bearing.

Case in point, my second ex-husband was one of the most vile people I think I have ever come across in my life. There are many reasons why and they are best saved for yet another different book.

When I left him, it took me ten long months in therapy to get over what he did to me. Needless to say, he committed heinous crimes and violated many people and he was definitely not all he was cracked up to be or made himself out to be. To be honest, I did well to stay with him the length of time I did. I don't regret many of our times together because I have Fred and I learnt to become the strongest version of myself. Despite that, he and I shared our own very different stories.

My ex-husband took me to the depth of darkness only reserved for outer space and made me shake hands with the Grim Reaper on more than one occasion; I ended up spending five long and incredibly difficult years with him. But, despite all that, I was the only person who he really opened up to and could allow himself to be that version of normal he saw himself being. He portrayed many different sides to his character and I wonder now whether that was because he came from a generation of repressed needs – sexually- and being surrounded by family who expected their children and siblings to act a certain why. Was it because anything other than 'normal' was seen as a weakness, therefore he had to present himself as the hardest person.

During our years together, he was aggressive both physically and mentally, violent in thought and actions, judgmental against anyone and everyone, bigoted towards everything and rude … The list goes on, however, he harbored a secret so deeply that he had convinced himself that he could blot it out and I'm assuming that by taking his frustration out on others it helped him cope with how he was feeling. Until I came along and started rocking his foundations.

Underneath all his exterior hard shell and at the very core of his underbelly, he was a secret cross dresser. In fact he had never told anyone not even his first wife. To the trained eye, all the signs were there, to the untrained eye, they wouldn't of even known, which probably helped him hide it. He had never allowed anyone to see that side of him and he had tried so hard to cover it up, to the point of ridiculing anyone else who showed those tenderizes or anyone identifying as LGBTQ+. He would also show immense disgust. It's one of the first tale tell signs of a secret closet bigot.

But along came little old me. Intuitive me. The people-watcher me. I worked it out very quickly and very early on in our relationship and went to great lengths to help nurture him. I didn't have too, he certainly didn't owe me anything nor I to him. But, it goes back to my own learnt behaviour of wanting people not matter who they are and what they have done to me, to feel happy with who they are when they are around me. I studied him with great intent when we went clothes shopping. I would watch him feeling all the lingerie fabric, trying to work out what it would feel like against his own naked skin. I would tease him and egg him on to feel the texture or material etc and watch him turn a shade of crimson.

In the end, I would go out without him and buy him clothes; I would look for high heels and tight dresses and skirts and even wigs for him, so that he could become this alter ego he had always wanted to be. I would sit and watched from the kitchen as he inspected the clothes laid out on the bed for him and how he would react. I even went as far as letting him dress in front of me. I really don't need to go any further with this.

I do wonder to this day, why he allowed himself to be free with me. Whether by doing so, it has allowed him to move on after us, to accept that part of himself that he needs so much I will never know, but I hope it helped him.

So, what has this got to do with my story? Well …

Despite the fact that I showed him great kindness and care with an issue that he held so deep and dear to him, fundamentally, it never changed him. You would think that anyone like him would start to show compassion towards anyone else, but he never did.

When Jack 'came out', my ex-husband turned vile. He was the most bigoted arsehole towards Jack. And it was heart-breaking and sole destroying to watch.

God alone knows why he was the way he was. I guess it was all about saving face in front of people. I purpose in his mind if he accepted it would it then open up his secret closest. Maybe it was to keep up the pretense of a rock-solid exterior by refusing to allow any cracks to be visible. Maybe he thought that he would discredit himself or lose people close to him? He had over twenty years of pretending to be this hard villain, laughing at others misfortune or hardship in some way. Bursting that bubble would bring his world crashing down around him. Or, maybe he was jealous of Jack for having the balls to chase a dream of happiness and he knew he didn't have the courage to do the same?

Jealous of chasing a dream.
Jealous of being happy.

Jealous of allowing himself to be who he needed to be.

He didn't take the news of Jack well at all. As I have already said, it ended up dividing us further. He would refuse to call Jack by his new name. He even refused to address him at all or even talk with him, let alone stay in the same room as him. When Jack entered a room, he would go to the extreme of laughing at him or making snide remarks about what he was wearing or doing or how he looked. So much so, that he took his behaviour to a whole new level when he knew Jack was working. At the time we lived where we worked so it was unavoidable that we would dump into each other.

He would go to the extreme of gathering his work colleagues and seek Jack out while working. They would all stand there pointing and laughing at Jack, just for the fun of it and in front of fellow staff members and on days where there were members of the public within ear- and eye-shot. It was disgusting to hear and see.

It amazed me how Jack coped with it, and he did, incredibly well. He was able to turn a blind eye and never let my ex-husband see that it got to him. It made him stand that much taller and that much prouder, which in turn got to my ex-husband even more. What's more amazing is the age and mental difference between a seventeen-year-old verses a forty-five year old. I on the other hand wanted blood. The red mist came down on me, as it would with any parent, but I couldn't react. Jack didn't want the extra hassle, he just wanted to get on with his job in the quietest way possible. So, I respected that. Karma has a funny way of kicking its heels and yes, pay back is a bitch.

What's more and most probably an even bigger twist that you couldn't have seen coming, was my ex's family. His eldest sister point blank refused to acknowledge Jack as Jack and ended up belittling him to his face whilst in front of me and on our own doorstep. Despite the age difference between the two of them, she was sixty, Jack smiled, thanked her for her rudeness, stood in front of her and turned to address me and ushered me off. He never once bit at their rudeness or bigoted attitudes and I am thankful for that. What I do struggle to deal with or understand, is the fact that my ex-husband was a crossdresser. I do think that he thought he could get away with it simply because he thought the children didn't know. By this point in our relationship, Jack did know. Which again does show the level of maturity he had by not once mentioning it or by making my ex feel like he was worthless or how he was trying to treat him.

We never gave the situation another thought or word after that, it wasn't warranted. It was disgusting behaviour from a woman in her sixties. Pride just doesn't come into it. How lucky am I to have a child who is so well balanced in his approach to everything.

There is yet another bigger twist. And if you didn't see the last two coming, you definitely won't see this one.

My ex-husband's brother-in-law, who has been married to his other sister for a lifetime (you would get less for murder), for what would be over forty years, both are seventy-plus years old and probably retired now, but he is an RAF veteran. He served in the RAF for over forty years. What a hero! What a legend! To serve Queen and country for that length of time. Or so you would think!

Let me change your mind on those thoughts. His sole job, sole purpose, the only thing that got him out of bed in the morning, the one job he was so very proud of … and in his own words,

"To whittle out the gays among the proper men!"

Yes, you read it right, his sole job was to infiltrate the RAF and to work out who was gay and who wasn't. Back in the day, and until recently, being gay in the armed forces, led to a court martial and being booted out, humiliated and mentally let alone physically dragged through the ringer.

But…..What's more, to add a huge insult to injury, he and his wife had an only child. A son, his pride and joy, his world-famous musician son. How he made them proud. And how was is openly and proudly GAY!

So karma really does come and bite you firmly on the arse when you least expect it. I think the lesson is most definitely, you reap what you sow.

It wasn't until after I left my ex, that I let my family including my children know what he was like. To say that it shocked them was an understatement. More to the point, it didn't help them understand why he behaved the way he did towards Jack or anyone else for that matter.

So why was he such an arse to everyone else? Obviously, he wasn't towards his nephew, he accepted him the way he was. Praised him, loved him, even to the point of showing him off to anyone and everyone that would listen.

I do think that if his nephew ever found out, he would be mortified or there may be a chance that he wouldn't even believe it of his uncle because he had never experienced anything like that whilst growing up. I don't think I will ever know but I do know that throwing stones in a glass house whilst you are under its protection is never a good idea. Particularly, if you have something of your own to hide.

Since we parted company, I do know that he has embraced a certain accept of being open with crossdressing. Not all the way, but it is a start. And as for his attitude towards anyone else that falls under the LGBTQ+ umbrella, who knows, stranger things may happen and he may be more open to being accepting of diversity.

CHAPTER 14: ONE STEP FORWARD, FIVE STEPS BACK …

2018 was packed full of ups and downs and sprinkled with many changes for everyone to deal with. I finally plucked up the courage to leave my now ex-husband. Which was very tough. But it did at least see a reconciliation between myself, my mother and brother for the first time in over five years.

I learnt that Jack had taken my advice and reached out to his uncle when I had mentioned it. For that, I was pleased. Whether he got the support or not at that time, or whether it hindered him, I don't really know. We never discussed in detail what they talked about. It was a private conversation between them and I didn't want Jack to feel that he had to tell me everything. But I do know I was right and maybe I shouldn't have suggested it. This will become clear as this story unfolds.

After we managed to regain some form of normality from moving and rearranging our lives, I took Jack to the doctors to formally start the transition process. The doctor we saw at our GPs practice was lovely; she was attentive to Jack's concerns and questions and gave us some hope that the western medical profession were adapting to changing times. We were informed that we couldn't do anything until he turned eighteen years old but that there were some things we could get started and in the pipeline for when that moment came. At this stage he would be able to go onto the waiting list to be seen by the NHS Gender Clinic. One of the first questions any health professionals ask when going through gender reassignment is, how long have you lived under your new persona. They are looking for people who have lived as they intend for over a year. Other areas that one would look to change could be hair, clothes, makeup and name change. These small and manageable changes all help to get that ball rolling.

Okay, so we had a way forward and we knew that he had time to prove that he had been living under his new way of life since July 2018. This would give him a clear six months plus. At the time, this proof was part of the criteria that the gender clinic would be looking for. If anyone attended the clinic without this proof, they could be turned away until they could prove it. A great shame for many people, but again, I do appreciate that not everyone's journey through gender reassignment has turned out the way that they had hoped. Some people have had their journeys reversed because of a lack of input from the medical profession.

Criteria, law and processes are changing all the time, anyone starting out on their own gender reassignment journey should seek up to date information. Thankfully Jack had done as much homework as possible to support us in getting the ball rolling. At the time of Jack's reassignment, everything but his passport had been changed and of course for those going through gender affirming surgery a passport at that time, couldn't be changed until top surgery was performed.

Pre 2020, there were two requirements needed: a letter from your doctor or medical consultant confirming that your change of gender is permanent, that you have attended two medical appointments and that you are stable in your actual gender role, together with evidence of your change of name, i.e. Deed Poll. However, to show how quickly processes are changing, there has been another change in the process at the time of writing this book, all that is required now is a letter written by the transitionee and the official deed poll certificate, which has aided the process to become more time saving and streamline.

During this time, Jack had begun to embark on a career in the Navy. He had completed seven years in the Sea Cadets, gained every certificate and qualification going, done everything they had to offer and finally reached petty officer's grade. As soon as he turned eighteen, he became staff. But, he didn't want to stop there, he wanted a life in the Navy so badly. After speaking with the Navy Office in his home county, he was informed that he had to go through the whole process again and as a new applicant. This involved filling out forms, attending the many interviews they asked for and conducting medical and physical examination. So, he did. Until the next stumbling block came up.

When he was seventeen, he made the call to the NHS Gender Identity Clinic (GIC). Please don't forget that this was only 2018. When he made the call, he was told that there was a two-year waiting list to GET ON TO the waiting list, which would then see another two years before he would be offered a consultant's appointment. Two years plus two years equals FOUR years in total before being able to see a consultant on the NHS! Are you having a laugh? What are people meant to do during that time. That would have made him twenty-two years old. That's not good enough. Not only are the people in this situation living with the difficulties of physically presenting themselves the way they need too in order to fit in and live their lives to the best of their abilities; they are dealing with the mental strain of their situation.

At the time of writing, I am flicking back between my web browser and manuscript, in utter disbelief. As of today, 6th October 2022, the current waiting time on the Gender Identity Clinic is sitting at nearly three years. They are currently working on referrals from January 2018! On the waiting list on this day, there were, 11,407 people. Only fifty first time appointments were being offered a month.

Jack's eighteenth birthday came and went. A milestone in anyone's life, more so for someone trying to transition. He was able to make contact with Transgender Clinic in London, who were a private clinic, where he was able to get the ball rolling.

I am thankful that Jack has had a network of people, supporting him during this process. We, as a family, understand this is not the case for so many others out there.

We have heard so many different stories through our journey, some are good and some are awful. Some transitioners have been alienated from their families, having their support network slashed to less than half and some have taken their own lives because the process is too lengthy and laborious. Whilst others have found support in unlikely places, which has been heart-warming to see and share.

As a family, we have seen people, and by people I mean, teachers, supply teachers, headteachers and dinner staff, not the children themselves, because the current generation of school children are more in tune and have greater understanding. But in education, those who are supposed to have our children's best interests at heart, often fail them. We have seen how sometimes the adults in education can be the least educated in gender issues and sexuality.

What I would say, is that the people closest to anyone going through transitioning or trying to work out which gender identity fits them best, are the only people that see the everyday struggles they go through. There are many struggles that others don't see or understand. From a workplace environment, school environment or simply down to the random people transgender people meet in the street. The backlash transgender people or anyone struggling with gender identity get from everyday people, who are uneducated and unwilling to see change or learn how to deal with it, can be mentally and physically damaging. When dealing with red tape, the walls in place can be insurmountable. To the transitioner, all they want to do is live a quiet life in the way that makes them happy.

There are many people who struggle with body dysphoria, I for one do and I didn't recognise that this was what it was. Or understand anything about it in real terms, until I watched what Jack was going through and talked to him about how he felt. I have coped with body dysphoria since I was nine years old to the present day, all thanks to my brother. But I am so incredibly fortunate that I am the type of person who turns a negative into a positive and I have been able to understand how Jack has felt and have acted to help him to the best of my abilities. Although I will add that no one will be able to fully understand what it must be like for anyone transitioning because, they aren't the ones going through it.

I understand more than anyone, what it is like to look at yourself in the mirror and not like the vision reflected back. To look at that reflection and know that it doesn't represent who you are inside. It has helped me to understand what Jack has gone through and is going through and it has helped me to understand how anyone in that position might be feeling; whether they class themselves as non-binary, gay, fat or thin.

All I would ask of you, the person reading this book: do you feel like that? Have you ever felt like that? Even in the slightest way and could you comprehend how it must feel? Stop and take a small moment out of your day, to just think about how that might feel. It took me twenty-nine years to realise what I was feeling and that there was an actual term for it. Suppressing all those feelings for twenty-nine years, which were imposed upon me from someone else.

Ask yourself if you have any idea what it is like, looking at your reflection and hating it with every ounce of your being?

Do you have any idea what it is like to walk around in a body that is one hundred per cent betraying you because it doesn't represent who you truly are?

Does a non-understander have any idea of what it would be like to walk just five steps in the shoes of someone who is trying to achieve their true self?

If they don't and if they don't have the capacity to begin to understand what the transgender person or anyone struggling with LGBTQ+ issues is going through. Then they don't have the right to say anything at all.

No one has the right to comment on someone else's struggles unless they are prepared to take the time to understand them fully. Anyone dealing with LGBTQ+ issues have their mental health turned upside down and inside out already; they don't need you adding to it anymore. What non-understanders say behind closed doors is up to them. It's important they learn to keep their opinions behind those closed doors and that they don't share them outside and with the general public.

I have seen first-hand the lack of support and failings of two institutions that are designed to help us, the NHS and educational system both need a massive overhaul. A re-education from their cores.

I have heard stories of GPs who have laughed in the faces of their patients. GPs are our first port of call in any medical situation. If even one of them behaves like this, then they should be held accountable for any actions that arise from their behaviour. I have seen the everyday challenges that people dealing with transgender go through. And it's not plain sailing.

There is simply not enough being done to help anyone going through this process. These are real people, feeling real pain, both physically, emotionally and mentally and not enough is done to support them. As a human race we should be ashamed. It is our own lack of not understanding that hinders this process and our ability to move forward.

Whether non-understanders choose to accept this or not, I would challenge anyone to dress in the opposite gender and spend a day or even a week trying to deal with what is classed as normal living, to see what transgender individuals come up against. Then and only then might they begin to scratch the surface of understanding what LGBTQ+ individuals face.

Our family has faced these same issues. Not only did we come up against my ex-husband's attitude and that of his family's but we have also had to face the poor attitude of someone much closer.

CHAPTER 15: PARENTING DOESN'T ALWAYS GO TO PLAN …

My first-born child, Arron was clearly not raised in a judgmental and bigoted family. Given our family history, we are an incredibly diverse and gifted family, yet he has unfortunately turned into a person that I can't allow in my life or that of my children's. It is by no means an easy decision to make, but it is a vital one. He has not turned into the young man that I had hoped for and I am deeply sad about that.

As a mother/parent, we never really stop thinking about our children no matter their age, their position in the world or their relationship status. And just because I don't talk to Arron, it doesn't mean that I have forgotten all about him. It is unfortunate that he takes great pride in profiting from inflicting insults and pain on everyone else, which is a great shame. I know it is nothing that I have done and it is nothing to do with the way he was brought up. We have always tried very hard to be an open family.

However, my biggest spanner in the works and force that I have been unable to fight against is that of my mother. She chose her victim wisely and preyed on his weaknesses. She is after all the biggest walking hypocrite and contradiction going.

She is a mother and a grandmother of two

transgender males, yet she has encouraged one of her grandson's, her eldest one to behave in a manner that is bigoted towards his own brother. Arron has insulted, vicitmised and laughed at Jack, both out of ear and eyeshot of his grandmother and within ear and eye shot of his grandmother. He has knowingly told his grandmother of his actions and we all have told her of his actions. Yet, she has done nothing to put a stop to it or turn the table to make him see that he doesn't do it towards his uncle so don't do it towards his own brother. In all honesty, it has broken my heart, not just for myself, but Jack and for Arron. It is shameful and I am ashamed of both my mother and Arron and it is totally disgraceful. There are no words to describe how it has made me feel, not to mention what Jack must think. Arron's actions most definitely shaped how Emily approached her 'coming out' to me and the rest of the world. She has forever remained fearful of Arron finding out. More to the point, what must Jack be thinking and feeling, knowing that his grandmother allows this behaviour yet his uncle has been treated completely differently and presents the same as him.

Over later years the mental strain which has been placed on me by Arron has become too much to bear. This toxic and untenable situation has spread over into my other children's lives. I suppose every family has a bad apple and it's how you deal with that apple that has a bearing on the rest of the family. Sometimes choices must be made which are heart-breaking but life saving and are done with the very best of intentions, regardless of how painful they are to execute.

Throughout Arron's life, he has always known that his uncle was transgender. I made the decision to tell him when he was seven. He was a bright child; he had semi worked it out by this point. I hadn't planned to discuss anything with the children, it was my life's mission not to. In fact, my brother had demanded that I didn't tell anyone.

Transgender was never a conversation I had with my mother or brother. My brother didn't ever ask how we would address the situation if the question of his transgender ever arose. It was very much a short, fast answer of, 'We don't need to discuss it, no one ever needs to know.' It made it very hard to know what to say.

Being a parent is a totally different ball game. I wouldn't be the way to start the conversation, but I would answer as honestly if I was ever asked.

Arron, who was seven years old at the time, had been looking through an old photo album, when he came across one photo with a female holding a baby and on the other side of the page another photo of my brother holding Arron as a toddler. He kept flicking between both photos and I could see him thinking; eventually he turned to me and said, "That looks like Aunty Sue?" I sat there stunned into silence, it wasn't a 'Who Wants to be a Millionaire question', I had no 50:50 answer, no phone a friend on speed dial, or ask the audience. I had to think quickly and decide which answer was for the best. I made a decision, led by example and tell the truth, big girl pants on and all that.

I felt backed into a corner and had to think quickly, so I decided to tell him what had happened and to start educating him. Arron asked lots of questions and there were some I couldn't answer but I managed to wing it enough. I didn't lie or sugar coat it. And that was that. I was worried that at some point Arron may just randomly blurt out everything we'd discussed when we saw them next, but it seemed it had been water off a duck's back.

At one pointed I braved telling my mother and explained how it had all come about. She immediately got on the phone to my brother, who in turn rang me straight away, hurling loud abuse down the phone to me. My mother was on the call too and she didn't step in to stop it or at least to try to be diplomatic about it. She didn't try to get him to see there was more than one point of view. I had no support from her at all. I was told I was stupid. My brother said, "It's not your place to tell them anything … how dare you tell your children anything to do with the situation." He stated that I hadn't asked for his permission to do so. My brother argued and shouted at me. He made me feel insignificant as a person and as a parent. However, I go back to my originally statement, he never gave me an alternative option and never discussed with me or as a family what the if's and buts could be.

I wanted my children to be well educated in all aspects of life. I wanted them to make sound choices and decisions but most of all, I wanted them to treat every human with respect.

However, despite my best efforts at having a casual

attitude and not making a big deal about this or any other situation surrounding gender or sexuality. Additionally, in my hope of raising a well-educated, well-mannered and inclusive son, it seems I had failed miserably.

Today, I can sit here, and honestly say, whole heartedly, that I know the underlying issue isn't actually me. It has taken me many years to recognise and retrain my brain into realising that it wasn't my fault. Deep down, you can't change a person. You aren't responsible for their actions, words or thoughts. You can only do your best and if it turns out your best is not good enough, then the issue lies with the other person.

I am ashamed to say that my eldest is a 'pick and choose' bigot, his dogmatist actions, words and thoughts are all aimed towards his siblings. Whether they are aimed towards anyone else, we shall never know, I haven't stuck around to find out, because I don't want to be tarnished with the same brush as him, nor do I want all my hard work with my other children to come undone. I just know that we have lived in the direct fire of his views.

He always grew up knowing that his uncle was transgender, yet he never had any issues surrounding this or raised any hint of unease. He grew up knowing my brother's names, both before and after his transition. He had seen before and after photos. And he refers to him as his uncle and has him listed on his phone as his uncle.

When he found out that his second sibling was preparing to start a new journey, he changed. His true colours showed through; he became hateful, crude, and bigoted. He started showing his hatred towards me. Later on down the line, in 2020, I worked out that behind my back my mother had been the biggest influence in his life. Pulling on vulnerable strings and twisting things in his head. She preyed on his vulnerability.

I also wonder whether he had picked up on how my ex-husband had behaved and liked the way he took pleasure in causing someone else pain? If all of this was fueled in the back of his mind with the twisted input from my mother? Maybe he was jealous in his own way but, from my point of view it became embarrassing for us all to deal with. It drove a massive wedge between us all. I simply wasn't going to stand for it and I hated the mental pressure he put on me. He would say that I should put him first because he was my firstborn child and therefore, he took precedence over the others. It's not fair for anyone to put that amount of pressure on anyone else, especially when it became clear that the issues lay with him and not anyone else.

He refused to have anything to do with Jack, from the moment he started to transition. He would walk out of the room if Jack entered. Or give him dirty looks when he was speaking, cooking or taking part in any family activity. He insisted on referring to Jack at all times as his sister, even if we were in other company; people who didn't know about Jack's journey. It was embarrassing and gut wrenching to watch and be a part of. It was just awful being in that situation.

We went through things like: his refusal to rename

Jack as a phone contact. He took great pride in telling him he had him down as his birth name and wouldn't be changing it. In the middle of the night and at random times he would phone him on a withheld number calling him a tranny, a loser and a nobody. Telling him that he, Arron, would do so much better in life than Jack would and would earn more money etc. It went above and beyond what you would class as normal sibling rivalry. He took immense pleasure from taunting and goading him. But, he wouldn't dare subject his uncle to the same treatment.

The bottom line is, it doesn't matter who you are; I will not tolerate behaviour like this towards any one of my family, even from a member of my family. I will simply cut you off. I have learnt to have no issue with this. It is my duty as a parent to do whatever it takes for the betterment of my family. My other children were watching and learning his behaviour. All my hard work over the years would or could have been ruined. Not to mention that at the time, I had another child struggling with their sexuality. One who was disappearing within themselves because of their fear of being subjected to the same treatment.

Even to this day, Arron doesn't know. How terribly sad is that? At the age of fourteen, Emily confided to me that she was a lesbian. She was terrified that Arron would find out. No one should be put through that amount of emotional agony, especially not from a family member when they are already going through a challenging time.

Having talked a great deal with her about this book

and its content, I naturally asked if she had any fears about approaching me at any stage. I think I would have been mortified if she had. Of course, she was nervous but she had been a huge part of Jack's transition and she knew deep down that she wouldn't have any concerns in telling us.

Despite having to cut Arron loose and having had the same done to me by my own mother, I know I am not my mother's daughter. She freely, willingly and happily cut me and my children from her life, not once but twice. On both occasions, her justification was the same, because it was the easier thing to do to keep my brother happy. She has knowingly denied all knowledge of having a daughter to anyone, as well as denying she has grandchildren on my side. If, she does tell anyone she has grandchildren, she tells them that I have brainwashed them into not wanting anything to do with her. But she forgets that her grandchildren have been privy to her behaviour and what she is capable of.

Despite this fact and knowing that I have had to break all contact with my eldest son – one of the hardest things I have ever had to do – I have not just walked away. From afar and without Arron's knowledge, I follow him on social media to see how well he is doing with his business and to see the crafts skills he is using. Additionally, I send him anonymous birthday and Christmas cards each year. I haven't totally forgotten him, like my mother has with us. Some people may disagree with me and question whether he deserves it or not, however, I am a different mother to my mother, I can't just forget, unfortunately I don't work like that. I wish I did, because it would be easier.

Going back to my other children and to show you the contrasts, Fred is the polar opposite to Arron. At the age of three and a half, his mental and emotional transition from having a doting sister to a doting brother was effortless. He didn't bat an eyelid; he accepted the change without comment or argument, without nastiness or finger pointing. Yes, you could argue that it was to do with his age and potentially how we dealt with it versus a brother who was older and had been through much more and who understood the ins and outs of everything in finer detail. But Fred went from having a family that consisted of three females and three males to two females and four males. All he cared about was that he was still loved and cared for in the same way.

Fred grew up watching myself and Emily, doing our hair and makeup, nails and dressing up in dresses and high heels. It was normal for him to sit and watch us and to get involved. He would often ask to have makeup or nail varnish put on him and why not? Makeup is not gender orientated. Who are we to tell him it's wrong for a male to have these things when he has been in and around them his whole life? It was and still is normal for him, not because he ever saw his own father as a crossdresser but because we never told him it wasn't designed for males or that he couldn't have it. We gladly adorned him in anything he asked for. We didn't make fun of him. We didn't laugh. It was his happy place and that was that.

The same can be said about being around and totally included within the LGBTQ+ world. He doesn't raise an eyebrow when we are with our close same sex friends. He doesn't sit there being weirded out if they hold hands or cuddle or kiss. He's grown up in and around it and it's all normal to him. A further example of Fred's upbring relates to a recent fast-food toy – these Christmas Elves had either light coloured or dark coloured skin tones, he didn't mention the difference. He played with and treated this toy with the same level of equality he brings to human interactions. He is the pinnacle of acceptance and I am so grateful for having a family that backs up a celebration of diversity.

Even after Jack transitioned, he never said no to Fred or laughed at him when he wanted to wear makeup or dress up in my heels or dresses and I think that has made the bond between the two of them even stronger. They both have a great understanding towards each other and to others. Even to this day, Fred still asks to dress up and have makeup put on him and he's just turned eight. I feel very fortunate that he has the freedom to be able to express himself without fear of ridicule.

Everyone deserves the right to live their life the way THEY see fit. It's not your life, it doesn't affect you in any which way once you are behind your front door.

And for those who brand themselves as keyboard warriors? They should be ashamed; hiding behind a screen and not having the guts to face their victims face to face, having said those hurtful words.

Even in the 21st Century, the human race lacks compassion and understanding on how to show respect towards anyone or anything, including themselves. We could do with learning so much from the animal kingdom; they don't judge or ridicule.

CHAPTER 16:
A BUMPY RIDE FOR ALL...

Following my exit from my marriage, I spent the majority of 2018, rebuilding my life, focusing on the children, finding a home and gaining further qualifications for my job. I did what was asked of me by Jack and I reached out to my mother and brother once I had left my now ex-husband.

Whilst it was nice to have the relationship back with my mother, to a certain degree, I was unable to let go of the fact that she had totally disowned my children for over five years. During those five years she had known too that I had been diagnosed with Deep Vein Thrombosis and Pulmonary Embolism's whilst being pregnant and despite this knowledge she didn't wish to reach out to me and see if I needed her.

She had erased all knowledge of myself and my children to the outside world. On its own, this cut like a knife; let alone what it must have felt like to the children. Once again we were thrown into the knowledge that there were no pictures of us or any reference to our existence in for home or life. However, there was one person she had stayed in contact with and without my knowledge. I had found out that she had remained in contact with Arron, wisely and cunningly dripping poison from her glass pipette into his mind. All he could focus on was what he thought were the wrongs I had done to him, twisted at the very core by my mother. He branded me as the worst mother possible. He called me the most awful names and twisted everything into something that never existed. Everything we had been through over the last few years had sealed my fate and she used that against me, time and time again.

During this time of getting reacquainted, I also learnt that I had a new nephew and the children had a cousin for the first time. He was also born in 2014, the same year as my youngest; and just three months before. My dream of the two of them becoming best friends was hopeful.

There are times when I wonder why my brother decided to go down the route of parenthood, but then that could be asked of any of us. Sometimes parenting is thrust upon us unknowingly and sometimes it is longed for but never comes. We all have a different path when it comes to parenthood and none of us enter into it thinking that life will change further down the line, leading us into a very different directions than the first one we thought we were heading into. However, my brother was not and is not built for parenthood. He is the spitting image of my father, far too selfish to be able to entertain someone else's wants and needs. He is also too jealous of anyone else getting attention when he is in the room and he is too selfish to have to give up his time to care for someone else.

Needless to say, he and his then wife, who was fifty at the time and a heavy alcoholic, embarked on parenthood. For obvious reasons they had to embark on a journey which some of us take for granted. They had to go down the route of IVF using both egg and sperm donors. This process is long, heart breaking, soul destroying and very expensive and I am sure there are many families in whatever form and shape who would have loved the opportunity of having a willing friend to help them.

At the early start of my brother's transition and when he started his hormone replacement therapy, he didn't opt for any of his eggs to be saved. By the time he and his wife decided to become parents, she was considered far too old at fifty to produce good eggs. Not to mention that they didn't know what if any affect her years of alcohol abuse would have had on her body. As I have already mentioned, regardless of what I was put through, I had always offered my services to either have my eggs harvested or to be a surrogate for him.

Not long after I found out about my nephew, I was speaking with my mother about the process and I reminded her that I had always been willing to be a surrogate for him. Her reply was one I was not prepared for. She told me that my brother didn't think I was good enough material for him to use for producing a child. There is nothing more that I can add to that sentence to convey how I felt. Even now, as I sit here typing it and remembering how it felt to hear my mother just let it roll off her tongue, as though it were water off a duck's back. For her to listen to those words coming out of her mouth; to not register the look in my face, still baffles me greatly. Not to mention that it reaffirms how worthless my family have always made me feel. In another discussion that I had had many years prior to this, my mother was so blinkered within her own thoughts that she honestly thought that one day not only will gender reaffirming surgery consist of a new appendix but a totally functional ball sack that will work as intended. I do believe that she thought my brother would be the first transgender male to have this procedure done. Such is their own importance!

Don't get me wrong, I know fully what is involved in producing a baby; I've had five of them. But I would have offered my services to so many couples and even to my own children if they had found themselves needing it and for no gain other than the look of love from those parents who had to wait a lifetime to feel the way I felt about parenting.

My grandmother taught me selflessness from an early age; how not to profit from someone else's misfortune. I have talked about it many times with our closest same sex friends and how I wished I could have given them a child; but sadly after going through the medical complications with his pregnancy and giving birth to , I am unable to have any more children.

The innocent party in all this is my nephew. He never asked to be born and he was only brought into the world through the selfish act of my brother and his wife. What's more, his existence has been built on a lie. My brother and his wife decided never to tell her family about his gender reassignment. To this day, they still believe that my nephew is the product of both parents.

Sadly, as I had already mentioned, my sister-in-law had spent many years as an alcoholic, brought on by the tragic and sudden death of her first husband.

I say selfish because it was. Her levels of alcohol dependence were very high and they had taken their toll over the years. However, my sister-in-law had managed to carry to full term and had managed to remain 'dry' throughout the entire time. Within days of having him, she returned to her addiction of alcohol which ultimately resulted in her having a catastrophic stroke which left her totally wheelchair bound just when he was about one year old. The withdrawal from alcohol for the nine months prior and the shock of pregnancy more than likely had a part to play in this devastating medical condition. She was selfish to even think she would be able to fully mother a child at her age and with her medical conditions.

The result of the stroke was too much for my brother and his wife and they ended up divorcing, which saw him and my nephew moving back in with my mother full time. This gave my brother the freedom to become an absent parent with my mother picking up the pieces. Let's not forget, she had raised her own family, that she had also never given me one ounce of help towards my children, yet she was the one left raising a baby in her late seventies.

I saw first-hand the pressure my brother put on my aging mother by demanding she help to raise her grandson. Right up until now, at the age of eighty-two, she is still running around caring for both of them. She gets my nephew up and ready for school five days a week, picks him up from school five days a week, feeds him, entertains him and gets him ready for bed. She is an elderly single parent whilst my brother is nowhere to be seen.

From 2018, when we were back in contact with them, we witnessed first-hand how he plays at being an absent father. He works all the time and not anywhere close by, then he's off seeing his new girlfriend. When he's not working, he doesn't spend much time with his son because he gets easily stressed and runs out of patience with him, so he palms him off onto anyone that will have him: school clubs, parents of school children, outside school clubs.

My brother should never have become a parent, he lacks the skills required to take on another human being's mental, physical and emotional needs over his own. He lacks the capacity to see anything other than his own point of view. He is a mental predator, constantly seeking out his next weaker victim. He is a danger to anyone's mental health, even the strong minded but especially those that are mentally and emotionally vulnerable.

Going back to the subject of his and his wife being non-biological parents, when I raised the subject with my brother and asked whether he was going to tell his son, I was shot down, scowled at and told to mind my own business. The bottom line is, my brother is not prepared to, nor is he ever planning to tell his son. I feel that is wrong, he has a right to know how he came in to this world. Not to mention the situation that would arise if he needed any medical help, and discovered that his own family aren't able to help him. How will that make him feel? Their relationship is already clearly very strained; this will just be added to over the years.

During the period from 2018-2021, we witnessed the effect my brother was having on his son; it was soul destroying. My brother spent years criticising me for my parenting skills, yet would not have anything bad said against his lack of parenting. Even my mother backed up what I was saying behind his back, but to his face she contradicted her words. Making me out to be the one who was being a bitch. He also made numerous comments about the fact that I have had children with different fathers. I never planned too and I never planned for my first marriage to fail, but it did and that's that. But to show how hypocritical my brother is, he has since married his new girlfriend and they have embarked on a new baby together, must probably at the expense of my mother. His girlfriend didn't want another baby, because she had another child before they met, who happens to be the same age as my nephew. It wouldn't surprise me if my brother bullied her into it because he was desperate for another child.

I have learnt that parenting is a skill you must acquire and grow into. No one asked to be on this planet, we are here through the selfish act of pleasure and the innate need to procreate. As a newly conceived fetus, we weren't given freedom of speech or asked for our consent before entry in to the world. If we knew we were going to be born into families that mistreated us, we would surely choose not to be born at all.

There's nothing wrong or right in wanting or not wanting to have children. Each decision is personal and whilst we are unable to foresee the future beyond the point where we become parents, the one aim no one should ever have is to fail their children in the most selfish way possible. Children have to and should always come first.

The road to parenthood is even harder if you identify as same sex couples, transgender people or have infertility issues; the same stigma surrounds them all – time and money. Seeking help through fertility clinics for whatever reason, is lengthy, expensive and for some people unachievable.

CHAPTER 17: **COVID-19...**

Just before Covid-19 took hold in March 2020, Jack had managed to get his first appointment with the London Transgender Clinic, a private clinic. By this point he was desperate and felt he could no longer wait for the NHS to come good on their waiting times. He had asked if I wanted to go with him and despite my hatred for London, I was not going to let him go to such an important appointment without proper support. I wasn't going to let him be alone. In fact, I felt very privileged that he asked me to accompany him.

Some months prior to this, I had started a new relationship which was totally unexpected. Both myself, Jack and Emily had been left scarred over the bigotry that my ex-husband and Arron had put us through. I decided the best course of action was not to mention anything to my new partner. I wanted Jack to feel safe and to be respected for the man he was and not to be blurred by anything from the past. I wanted my new partner to accept Jack as my son before anything was mentioned.

I have never been ashamed or fearful of telling anyone I have a transgender child; I am so open and so proud of him. Sometimes I wish I could shout it from the roof tops, but I realise that I can't do that. If I had one hope or wish, it would be that everyone going through gender reassignment lived in a world where they could voice their experiences without fear of judgement or persecution from anyone else. That they had pride in their achievements which they held dear to them.

My partner offered to travel with me on the train, knowing I suffer with anxiety going to big busy places such as London. He saw us on to the road where the clinic was and then left us to seek out a coffee shop. Nothing more was said about where we were going or who we were seeing.

Everyone in the clinic was lovely, warm and so welcoming, which helped to put both of us at ease. We didn't have to wait too long before we were called downstairs to see the doctor. A lady doctor who was so much younger than me. Inwardly I was asking myself how she could possibly understand what someone in my son's situation was going through, but I was proved wrong. She was kind, caring, attentive in her approach, listening to Jack and his concerns, wants and needs. We spent over an hour discussing everything in great detail and she put both our minds at rest.

At the time of the appointment and whilst discussing how much surgery would cost, we were not in a financial position to support him through it. I wanted nothing more than to be able to support him but I couldn't find a way to do it. Everything comes at a cost, and when looking into this level of surgery the cost is even greater.

I do remember Jack saying to me while we were in the appointment, that he wished I was more like his grandmother, she had drummed it in to the children that I had to be do everything possible for the children and if I hadn't or couldn't she made me look and feel like a failure. She would happily remind everyone of the things she paid for and how she was able to pay for everything needed for my brother's transition. I won't lie, his tone and words cut me like a knife and hurt beyond words. I was very taken aback because I could see the disappointment in his face. I composed myself and gently reminded him that my mother was in a financial position to be able to pay for everything, but she had taken out a very heavy loan, over £120,000, to help pay for the surgery my brother needed. Twenty years ago, this type of surgery was cheaper and the NHS was more able and capable to deliver on time with other parts of the surgery – which was funded by them. Times had changed, costs had changed and because of the financial state I had been left in by my ex-husband, I wasn't able to take out a loan or help put any money to one side for him. If, I had been in the right position, I would have already signed the cheque.

We talked about cost in the appointment and the doctor turned to us after seeing Jack's disappointment. She picked the pen off her desk and pointed it straight at him.

"What you have in this room at this moment, is the full love and support of your mother. I've been doing this job for ten years now and I can honesty tell you that over 90% of the people that come through my door, do so on their own. Their friends and family have totally disowned them and they are facing this whole process entirely on their own. The fact that your mother is sat right next to you, supporting you, is priceless and don't you forget it." She turned away to carry on writing out his notes and a prescription.

A single tear rolled down my face and Jack grabbed my hand and squeezed.

"We'll find a way don't worry."

I think at that moment the penny literally dropped for him and he realised what he had in me and the rest of the family. He had a school friend in the same year going through the same process, male to female. I remember very well how her family took the news. A person's wealth is not measured by their success or possessions, it is measured by what they hold dear and what is irreplaceable to them. We may not have an endless pot of money or success but what we do have is a very close-knit family who supports each other, not just in their hour of need but all the time and the knowledge that we all have each other's backs.

We left the appointment with a prescription to start hormone replacement therapy which we would have to pay for privately, together with a plan for when surgery would start. Typically, you can have surgery without needing to go on HRT or if HRT has been started, surgery can take place then after two weeks. I think we both felt a sense of relief, we had a way forward. Going through the NHS was proving to be years away.

This time also allowed us to work out how we were going to afford the first rounds of surgery. Jack's double mastectomy alone was going to cost £7,000, but having spent the last fifteen years living on a budget, we were able to come up with a plan. We were able to save for the deposit and pay the rest on a credit card which would then be repaid by Jack. Not the best, but it worked for us.

This new treatment plan also gave him hope for being able to join the Navy. His career plans had also been stalled because of the NHS. Anybody going through the NHS for this type of treatment was literally having to put their lives on hold. It just felt unacceptable. His cadet training had shown he was born for a life in the Navy, he was made for it and he had been denied it by lack of funding in the NHS.

We met up with my partner and found somewhere for a quick bite to eat before parting and going home.

Nothing much was said other than that we had a way forward and that it would take time. We went on to talk about Christmas and holidays and before we knew it, it was time for the train. We made our way back to Kings Cross and exchanged cuddles and handshakes, before Jack boarded the train back home and we boarded our train which was going in the opposite direction. The long distance between us can sometimes be hard to manage but we work round it. One day we will move back up to where Jack is, but for now we will remain two and a half hours apart.

When I told my partner that I was writing this book, I asked him if he would like to add anything from his own perspective. He jumped at the chance, with the thought that if it helped just one person, he would be happy and as follows:-

"Jessica and I first met in the August of 2019. At first, we were just friends who would talk about everything and anything in the months leading up to Jessica's move in late October 2019, which would see her take a better job role. Jessica was in the middle of trying to piece her life back together after a turbulent time, so there was no mention of us becoming more than just friends. However, we stayed in touch and our friendship grew.

Jessica had always presented her children as four sons and one daughter; although her relationship with her eldest son, Arron, was very strained. Having read this story once she had finished it, it all made sense. I understood why she had handled it the way she had – and who could blame her. In truth I would never have known anything unless she had mentioned it sooner.

February 2020, finally saw Jessica and myself making our relationship more permanent. In the following month, Jessica mentioned that she was going to London to meet with Jack for an appointment. She didn't mention what kind of appointment but I knew that she didn't like to travel to London, so I offered to accompany her. At first, she was hesitant and a bit nervous, not only would it be the second time that I would be meeting Jack, but I'm guessing she was nervous because of the type of appointment it was. She never told me and I never really asked.

When we arrived and we met, I offered my hand and

received the firmest of handshakes, which I was always taught says a lot about a person, that they are genuinely pleased to meet you; that put me at ease. We talked as we walked; thanks to the London traffic and transport, time was ticking and we had to race across town.

When we reached the street, I left them to go in and went off to find a coffee shop about five minutes away. Not really thinking anything of the street we were on, I ordered a latte and sat thinking that I hoped I had made a good first impression. It hadn't crossed my mind as to why Jack had an appointment at a London clinic.

A couple of lattes later and I thought it was time to walk back, they were already out and heading towards me, so we about turned and headed to a little place where we could get a sandwich. We then sat and talked properly for the first time. I remember listening to them catch up with one another as though they hadn't been apart for months. Before we knew it, it was time to head back to the railway station. Jessica and Jack hugged and then he turned and gave me another firm handshake and we went in our separate directions.

We found our train and I waited until the train was in full motion before asking Jessica what her thoughts were, thinking for some reason that with the train in motion she would have less chance to run away. Jessica asked what I thought of her son, explaining that there was something she wanted to clarify with me. I said he seemed a genuine person who gave a firm handshake but also seemed to be his own person with his own thoughts. I guess that in hindsight he was a person going out to get what he wanted in life.

I would like to think that I am an open minded person, I have two sons and I love them unconditionally but I appreciate that nothing is black and white. But I didn't appreciate that a person could wake up not feeling happy with themselves; to the point of hating the person looking back at them. Other than hating our looks, which is something that we can all have deep down, we can always have our off days. It was something I never had to think about. But from that moment on, my whole outlook on life and people changed and that is all down to Jessica and her approach and handling of the situation. She has helped open my mind to what goes on and why.

Over the following months, we met and talked more with Jack. He would come down as and when he could and we would go up to him.

Like I said, he changed my opinion and respect for so many people who I had met and have yet to meet. To have the bravery, if that is the right word to use, to know that you want to change something about yourself and have the courage to go forward and then change it is an amazing quality. A quality that not everyone has, no matter what it is about their life that they desperately want to change."

CHAPTER 18:
A LONG AWAITED DAY...

The day had finally come. After waiting what seemed an eternity, the future Jack had longed for was now in grabbing distance. Three years from 2018 to 2020 was, and is, a lifetime for people in Jack's situation. His whole life had been on hold – waiting for this moment.

He had made the journey down to stay the night with us before journeying to the London Transgender Clinic the following morning. My partner drove us straight to the door and left us to go and check in at reception.

Honestly, I couldn't tell you who was more nervous and excited, me or Jack. I think for both of us, with so much going through our minds that so much had been pinned on this one defining moment.

We were shown into his room, which as you would expect was clean and clinical. The wait seemed to last for hours, but in truth, they had asked that he arrive only a few hours before needing to go down to theatre. At this time, the world was still in the throes of dealing with Covid-19, which had such a massive impact, following the first national lockdown. There was a sense of urgency in getting this operation ticked off the list.

Those few hours allowed us to have moments of reflection. I saw how excited he was at the thought of starting a new life in a new body, even if in reality it was the same body but just slightly modified. And I saw how nervous he was at the thought of having a major operation. The only other operation he'd had a few years prior was one to remove a tooth. Going from having a tooth removed to having a double mastectomy was quite a jump.

I remember the moments leading up to him going down to the anesthetist's room, we were talking, trying to calm our nerves. I had told him that I had spent the last three-years watching him and how when he woke up from surgery, he wouldn't need to do either ever again.

My other reflection was one that you may not have thought about. I was jealous of him. So incredibly jealous, but not in the way you may think and certainly not in a horrid way. I was born a woman, and with that comes certain ideologies, especially from the older generation or from misogynists of both genders, but also manmade ideologies. Many men have sexualised women and their body parts. At some stage as I entered puberty, I would have a pair of breasts to clearly define that I was a woman. In the eyes of misogynists, all women were good for was having babies and playing the part of being a good housewife; to be ogled over and objectified as nothing more than a plaything men could use as they felt they needed to. We were often seen as nothing more than a piece of meat. We are very rarely seen as anything else over someone of intellect or over a good businessperson or of being able to act or fend for ourselves.

I was brought up in a household where my father was

very strict on us and who desperately tried to keep me under his thumb. We were nothing more than a hinderance to him; our downfall was the fact that we were not males. I was to be seen and not heard. I was not allowed to think for myself or know my own mind. I watched him keep my mother at bay. She was the businessperson – the brains behind his work – yet she was kept in the background and never given any credit for her input, not to mention that my father never praised her in front of clients or dared to admit that a woman was running the business.

I'm sure that ninety-nine per cent of women want to be able to wear what they want without fear of some pervert thinking he has the right to look, see and touch. Women are not free to walk down the street topless, as men are. Men have breast tissue, just as women do; men also have nipples, just as women do, yet it is man who has made it impossible for women to be treated as equals. On the flipside, we are subjected to viewing shirtless men who could be viewed as distasteful walking around without a care in the world, yet it is perceived as acceptable, because society has made it that way.

Sitting here writing these thoughts down, I am drawn to how the western world has prided itself by even classing and identifying itself as being a modern civilisation, yet here we are and no, we aren't. If you look at ancient tribes predominately from Africa, they have not sexualised the female body, they have not objectified breasts and how they are presented in their community. Tribal women are able to walk about and conduct their business without the fear of radical treatment or persecution. So why has the western world brought this in and why do they think they have the right to strip women of the same rights which they give freely to men?

I wanted and still want, to be taken seriously as an equal person, but even now society has made it so hard for women to be taken seriously alongside their counterparts. By having our breasts removed, would it give the air of validation women seek? Could we get away with wearing a three-piece suit in the same manner and still be taken seriously?

My other jealous thought ran in parallel and was one of being able to recreate myself and start again. There have been so many times in my life when I have wished that I could erase myself and start all over again, blending into the background. Like a true Phoenix. I had crashed and burned many times and always wanted to rise up anew. Jack was being given the opportunity to do just that. He walked in through those doors as he was and would be leaving as a whole new person on the outside. How many people truly wish they could do that? Start all over again, with a fresh sense of perspective and clear direction.

My jealous thoughts didn't last long; I'm not naturally a jealous person, especially towards my children. The knock at the door came and we both walked down the corridor to the closed glass door.

He turned to me and said, "Don't start." "I'm trying my best not too," came my reply, through a half smile and a semi screwed-up face. We hugged the biggest hug and off he went. It doesn't matter how old you are, turning back to get that one last look of reassurance from your mum means the world.

I left him in the capable hands of the medical team, thinking to myself as I walked back down through the corridor that they had better not hurt my baby. I went through into the waiting room to be greeted by my partner who saw the look on my face and rushed to embrace me.

"Everything will be fine, you'll see. Let's grab something to eat."

I don't think I have ever clock watched so much in all my life. Here was me, thinking, stupidly that half an hour would be adequate time to perform what they needed to do; so I made us rush, just so I would be in there when he came round. I fully appreciated how expectant fathers felt, when they had to wait outside the birthing room for hours on end many years ago, before society changed the thought process on how that was handled. I was pretty sure two babies could have been born in the time we waited and I'm sure a whole season went past too.

CHAPTER 19:
A NEW START ...

Finally, after what seemed many hours later, a nurse strolled leisurely through the doors to inform us he was in recovery and asking for me. I'm fairly certain I didn't leave any tire marks when I got up; I had no clue where I was going but I was going.

He was in a lovely quiet recovery room, just him and the undivided attention of the nurses. I tentatively went over to him, thinking he was asleep and held his hand. At the touch of my hand, it made him jump, eyes wide open, which in turn made me jump.

"Don't do that! You scared me." Not knowing whether to cry or poke him, nearly collapsing at the side of the bed.

This mischievous smile came across his face and all I got was, "How you doin'?" in the best Joey from *Friends* voice. All the nurses giggled as they attended to him.

"Cheeky one here, I see," said one of the nurses.

A half-cocked smile just beamed up from the bed, still in and out from the anesthetic.

Once we established that he needed the toilet and that I was to help him, the reality set in. He had meters of wires and tubes coming out of him. Drains here and drains there, not to mention his very fetching DVT stockings. But from the moment I clapped eyes on him and vice versa to when we actually got him home, he had us in stitches. I don't think I've laughed so much when trying to be so serious.

All jokes aside, it's a major operation, which shows the dedication transitioning people are prepared to go through. Would you knowingly have a major operation just to change something? Knowing what the cost is all round?

In the meantime, and during the wait before being allowed to go home, we were shown and talked through everything we needed to do or to watch out for. We were given the emergency phone numbers and a huge bag of drugs containing anti-inflammation, muscle relaxants, antibiotics and painkillers.

Finally, we were given the green light and sent on our merry way. By the time we left London it was gone 9pm; at least the roads home would be quiet. Well, whilst the roads and some of us in the car were quiet, one of us was being their entertaining best. I remember the drive home; it was the funniest three hours I think any of us have ever had whilst stuck in a car. Jack kept going on about the two of us getting married; how he wanted to be invested so he could marry us. In true Joey from *Friends* style, we had his version of the giving and receiving speech over and over again.

We were heading for my mother's house. I had thought it best that Jack stayed there, simply because at the time we didn't have the space for him to rest and recuperate properly and I didn't want his younger brother jumping all over him. It had nothing to do with whether I thought my mother would do a better job or not. It went without saying that she wouldn't.

However, it didn't stop her reveling in the glory of playing nurse and having all the attention on her, just like she had done when my brother went through the same operations. It was almost as if she loved having to explain to people; to make her look like such a martyr.

Before I was even out of the door my mother, and especially my brother, had taken over and were telling Jack what to do and how to do it; how to sit and how to hold his drains properly. It was with a heavy heart that I left him and he knew it but he persuaded me he would be okay. Once I got him settled, I reluctantly left Jack there and we made our way home.

After a few days of going backwards and forwards and spending as much time as I could with him, it was time to change the dressings. I had phoned him on the morning we were going over to check that he was up and that everything was ready for us. Jack had asked me to change the dressing for him, which I was more than happy to do. By the time I arrived, my brother had already done everything. I wasn't allowed to get a word in edgeways, he belittled me again, in front of Jack, saying, "that I had no experience in doing anything like this and that I couldn't possibly do it to the level that he could." As always, my mother sloped off to the kitchen playing dumb and pretending to not hear anything.

The long and short of it is, both my mother and brother forced Jack into doing something he didn't want to do or felt comfortable doing, which demonstrates just the type of people they are. I won't say any more on this, you've probably gathered that so much of my life and events had been stolen by the pair of them. They seemed to take so much pleasure and pride in stripping me of what they think are key moments in my life. But they have sadly misjudged it.

A few days on from the operation, Jack had to go back to London for his check-up. We went up by train because he would be travelling back to his home after the appointment. I carried his bag for him while he tucked both his tubes and drains into the pockets of his coat. I could see him grimace every time he moved in his seat, or someone bumped into him. I just wanted to cover him in bubble wrap and get him to the clinic as quickly as possible.

We made our way across London via the underground and walking, which seemed to take an age but we made it to the clinic in good time. Although, I was semi prepared for what I was going to see once the dressings were removed. I wasn't prepared to see the extent of the drains. For those of you that haven't seen what it's like after a double mastectomy, the wounds are huge. They span the whole of the chest area, like two smiling faces looking at you, he didn't have a big chest area as it was. Those scars would be lifelong. After the healing process had finished they wouldn't look so red and inflamed, they would eventually calm down but they will always serve as a constant reminder. I see them as no different to a tattoo, those of us that have them, have had them for some reason or another. They map our journey through life. They tell our story without words.

I'm not a squeamish person at all, I have raised five children and I have worked on many equine yards with grim injuries, but I'm not going to lie, I did nearly pass out when they removed the drains from him. For a start, they were metal, secondly, they were about six inches or so long and thirdly, they helped to drain away any fatty tissue or excess fluid, which his contained. How he had managed to move with two of those in him? God alone knows. No wonder he was grimacing.

Once he was checked over and given further after care advice, we were sent on our way.

He needed to be careful not to rip the stitches open, so he wouldn't be able to do any heavy lifting at work. At least he would be able to go back to the Navy office and get the ball rolling with his application.

We made our way to a nearby café for some lunch, before heading in separate directions. I remember talking to him about everything and anything and how exciting the next stage of his journey would be. Getting him into the career he wanted was high on this list.

Despite his pain and clear discomfort, I remember watching him and knowing in my heart he had made the right choice. His confidence had grown even more. It was an immensely proud time for me as well as being exciting.

There were no two ways about it, the healing time and his road to full recovery was not going to be easy. He had to lessen his stubborn side and learn to take commands from others instead of dishing them out. We parted company, both of us sad to see each other leaving but excited for the next stages.

He had done as he had said he would and taken a few extra days off before heading back to work. In that time, he had managed to discuss options with the Navy office.

One step forward and a thousand back. His whole world came crashing down. After everything he had put in place, they refused him. Despite the fact that he'd had gender reassignment surgery and had now been officially allowed to change his passport and birth certificate, it wasn't enough. The Navy Office had changed the goal posts. They now said that they wouldn't look at accepting him until after he'd had the hysterectomy, due to the recovery time, which could be up to six months. They wouldn't invest in someone who had to take up to six months off due to surgery, within a year of signing up. How backwards can an archaic institution be? I wonder how other people within the armed services cope when they have to have surgery or rehabilitation due to injuries sustained at work?

Going private for the double mastectomy came with a price tag of over £7,000. In theory, because we had paid for this surgery, the NHS should have picked up the hysterectomy and it should have been done within a timely manner following the start of HRT and reassignment surgery. As always, there was an ever growing waiting list. Likewise, Jack is unable to have further corrective surgery until the hysterectomy is done. If we were to see him go private again a hysterectomy would cost upwards of £7,000 and a phalloplasty (penis construction) would cost upwards of £40,000 to £70,000.

Regardless of his age now, he has missed out on over four years of serving in the Navy. It was his chosen career and one that being part of the Sea Cadets proved he was incredibly talented at. They have no idea what they have missed out on. To say that it crushed him would be an understatement. He has lost his passion for the water and all that he has worked so hard for.

It's not in Jack's nature to let anything get him down. Although I know he misses a life in uniform, he's had to pick himself up and dust himself off and we are all proud of him for that.

Covid also had a part to play in the delays the NHS have had and still face. For how much longer will transitioning people have to wait to get on the right path and why aren't they seen as a high priority group?

CHAPTER 20:
JEALOUSY OR ENVY ...

Shaun, Emily, Fred and myself, made the move across four counties, to start a new life close to my mother and brother in 2019. After spending a year putting my life back together and studying, eventually passing a higher qualification for the role of local government officer. A job I'd had since 2016. This new qualification meant that I could go from working across five local authorities to just one and I would triple my salary. It seemed like a no brainer, despite my deep reservations about my mother and brother.

My decision was also cemented by the fact that I would effectively be moving back to where I had been born and spent the first half of my life. It brought back some harsh memories for me.

But, not one to be stopped in my tracks, I decided that I would give it a shot and give playing happy families with my mother and my brother a go. The children had been without any grandparent figures in their lives for years and seeing that my mother was the primary carer for my brother's son, her grandson, I thought it would be a perfect time for us to join in.

It meant that at least one of my children would be included within my nephew's life too and the pair of them would grow up having someone their own age to hang out with. I stupidly thought that I might have got some of the same support with childcare that my brother was getting. Seeing as I had been without it since I became a mother myself. My mother had always refused to help me out when I needed childcare even whilst we lived on her doorstep. I thought she would have liked or even maybe have wanted to at least try to make it up to me and to her grandchild. Ohhh … how wrong could I be. Silly me, I forgot that my brother was her first and foremost most important person and that I was just the tag along and annoyance to her.

Jack didn't make the move with us. He decided to stay where he was, as this had been the place where he had lived for over half his life. As much as I hated it, he needed to find his own way and I respected that, I might not have liked it, but I knew he needed to do it. I knew we all had a strong relationship with him, which wouldn't change. He stays with us as much as possible and we all missed him immensely when he wasn't with us.

Now, when I left my ex -husband and Jack made contact with my mother, this was when things shifted a bit. Once she knew he was going through transitioning he became her new favourite person. You might guess where this is going.

When he did stay with us and we paid my mother a visit, she would always make a fuss of him, telling him repeatedly in front of the other children and my brother, just how much she thought of him and how he was her favourite, without a care in the world. She wasn't shy in telling in saying it out loud. I wonder if she ever thought of the affect that would have had on the others?

It wasn't long before I could see how this was affecting my brother. After all, he had her all to himself for since 2001 and now he was being forced to share her with not only the one person he hated the most, that would be me, but another usurper who was stealing his limelight. Another person that was the same as him, which meant he wasn't unique anymore.

In his eyes, he was the elite one. He was the only person allowed to be special and to need superior treatment or attention. In his head he deserved the full spotlight and he wasn't going to give that up without a fight.

My brother was fixated on the relationship between myself, Jack and my mother. It was like watching a cartoon character from the good old days of Tom and Jerry, head spinning, steam coming from his ears and nose. Some would say it was comical to watch but if you knew the reason behind it then you would find it sad and pathetic.

There is twenty-four years between the two of them but Jack is the one who acted more maturely than his uncle. Jack always acted with grace and respect, putting to shame how badly behaved his uncle was. In a way, it was lovely to watch and be a part of but in another way, sad and very tiring.

Over the years, prior to all this, both my mother and brother would often tell me I was making it all up and that none of what I said and pointed out had ever happened. It was all part of that cycle of emotional abuse. The children were too young to witness the full extent of what I went through, so seeing someone else going through it, reaffirmed it in my mind. It wasn't made up, it did actually happen. My mother and brother were as bad as each other. If anything, I had learnt to cope with it better and had started finding my voice and calling them out when they did things and putting them on the spot in front of people. I didn't just stand there and allow it to all unfold. I wasn't going to be my mother.

At the start of Jack's transition, my brother would offer advice to him on things like which clinics were the best to go too and which surgeons to use and who not to use, what treatment he should be going for and what he needed to be doing etc. But what my brother didn't realise was, Jack was stubborn. If, he didn't want to do it, he wouldn't. If he wanted to find his own way, he would. And he wasn't about to be told least of all by his uncle.

However, my brother didn't see it like that. He self-importance and sheer arrogance shown through and he demanded that Jack listen to him. He had gone through the process nearly twenty years before and he knew best, not to mention that he was now a Doctor and therefore he was an act of God himself. To quote Shakespeare, "Time and tide, wait for no man."

Medicine and medical advances change on a daily basis and the advice he was giving Jack was outdated and not relevant to him. When my brother had started the process, gender reassignment surgery and treatment was in its infancy. It was just at the turn of the new century and gender reassignment was only just coming to the forefront of the medical profession. Surgeons he saw then had probably retired or worse passed over and practices had most definitely changed and even improved.

Jack had to and needed to learn his way, he had to feel comfortable in his own choices. After all, he had to live with them and not anyone else. But the more Jack appeared not to listen and to go his own way, the more it would frustrate my brother and the angrier he would become. Another person that made my brother's blood boil other than myself. At least I now wasn't on my own. In just over a year, the end of their relationship was on the cards and my brother refusing to have anything to do with Jack. The only one positive element that came out from this was the fact that at the very beginning of reacquainting with them, and pushing my own feelings to one side, I told Jack that speaking with his uncle would be best all round. Regardless of what my brother had done to me, I put myself to one side hoping for the best result. I think secretly, I always knew the breakdown would happen but I was putting Jack first and foremost at the front and recognised that I may not of been the best person to help him, which went against not just a parental intuition but a maternal one too. Every mother wants to be that person their child turns too and I had to fight that for Jack.

To prove just how bad it got, in Christmas 2020, after a long first year of Covid-19 restrictions, we had arranged to spend Christmas at my mother's. against my better judgement.

Why?

Even I don't know! I knew how it would pan out.

We had arranged that Jack would come down and spend Christmas with us at my mother's and that we wouldn't tell her nor my brother (big mistake). We kept it secret and planned around Jack and his work schedule. We had decided to drop as much of the food and bags round on the day before Christmas Eve, to help fit him in the car. Somehow she didn't twig. We then arrived properly at her house on Christmas Eve and shut the door behind us. Whilst all the greeting was going on, and the two youngest children were running around excitedly, my brother casually and nonchalantly made his way down the stairs and as he did so, there just happened to be a knock at the door. My mother became all flustered and rushed to answered it. We moved out of the way to allow her to take in the full surprise. Well, she screamed and jumped for joy when she saw Jack. She was in total shock but so happy to see him, making such a fuss over him.

We all turned to my brother who was going a lovely shade of red in the face, changed his stance on the stairs and went spare at Jack's unannounced arrival. He even had the audacity to spout Covid restrictions and demanded that he do a Covid test, telling him he had no right in being there and shouting that he had to wash his hands and had he worn a mask on the train etc? Coming from a man who had broken every Covid-19 restriction going during lockdown, this became a question of calling him the kettle or the pot.

To say the least, he was not happy would be an understatement. It was bad enough that he had to spend the Christmas with us in the same house but he hated the idea of another person in the house who would take away what he thought was his unreserved attention from his own mother.

Over the course of the previous two years, my brother had grown to dislike Jack as well as Fred, but Jack especially, because he was taking his place. He was the new kid on the block. The newcomer. The one who would be taking all the attention and having state of the art surgery with new and better techniques, ones they hadn't had all those years ago. Jack was living in the moment of going through the same process as my brother, but his experience was fresh and present in everyone's eyes and minds. This automatically qualified him to become my mother's favourite. She would be reliving memories of when my brother was transitioning and it was her chance to become a martyr all over again.

Over the course of the first hour, my brother became more and more angry. In the end, he turned into a petulant child, stomping round the house, slamming this and slamming that, making it quite clear he was not happy at the new and unannounced arrival or even with having a house full at all.

Eventually, and after doing our best to ignore his behaviour and trying to get him to take part in Christmas festivities, which he clearly didn't want to be part of; he took himself upstairs and went to sleep. His actions and mood set the tone for the rest of Christmas Eve, Christmas Day and Boxing Day. I've never been so pleased to be out of a house as I was that Boxing Day. I had spent three whole days cooking three meals a day for nine people without any help. I made it very clear then that I would never spend another Christmas in the same house as him; he's not a patch on Victor Maldrew!

It wouldn't be long, following the unfortunate events of that Christmas, that once again, my brother started putting his parts on and making demands on my mother that he didn't want us '*hanging around*'. Looking back at that time it all seems so clear. The contradictions and doubts my brother would sow in my mother's head, slowly turning her.

Covid-19 had brought many issues to the surface and my brother didn't like the fact that I challenged him and his actions behind his back. It was then that I started seeing how much power he held over my mother and how willing my mother was to accept it.

Towards the end of 2021, my brother had convinced my mother to sell her home and put all her funds with his and to buy a home which would solely benefit him once she passed. Within a month of them moving in together, his grip on her had tightened and it would be the last time we saw her or my nephew. We had popped round to help them with some electrical items, when my brother started an argument with me. He squared up to me within nose touching distance, spat in my face whilst shouting at high pitch at me, so much so that his face turned beetroot. My partner did the most obvious thing and stood up to him. Which was both of our downfalls.

I'm afraid I walked out and refused to be apart of anything anymore. He had stepped over that line and showed me what he was truly made off.

For the second time in my life and that of my children's, my mother had cut us off and dropped us like hot potatoes. She didn't even want to listen to our side of what had happened and she once again disowned us all as her family, never to be spoken of again, unless she was making us out to be the worst people ever and that it was all our fault. The only member of my family she and my brother have kept in touch with is Arron. Because they both knew they could manipulate him and drip poison into him, metaphorically speaking.

In hindsight, I and the rest of my family have felt nothing more than a sense of relief; we have never been happier and more settled.

As I have drafted this book and looking back on everything in finer detail, it has highlighted to me the extent of the abusive relationship with both my mother and brother that I was in. That, in fact, both of them knew what the other was doing, yet never stopped it. This is further backed up by my actions; as with any victim stuck in an abusive relationship, the victim always goes back for more, believing and hoping that there will be change. Sadly that change never comes.

Fortunately, there have been things that I have learnt along the way. One is how quickly my mother turns on my brother and confirms what she has been witness to; yet she denies it as soon as my brother knows. And another, is that my mother plays both the victim and the organ grinder; she has instigated and encouraged all of my brother's actions and that of Arron's. It has shown me that I not only have a brother who dislikes me but that my mother does too.

CHAPTER 21: THE JOURNEY CONTINUES ...

I am so deeply proud of Jack for having the courage and grace to accept that he needed to transition and with the way he has gone about it. I want Jack and any other person going through gender reassignment to remember where they came from; embrace it and treasure it. It's vitally important. It's your journey and it had to start somewhere.

Each person transitioning will have started their journey on one path and, whilst travelling that path, they have recognised and made a conscious decision to change paths for their mental and physical wellbeing. For Jack, his journey is by no means over. He is still very much in the throes of dealing with everything and trying to achieve his desired outcome.

Through this whole process and wanting to support Jack as best I can, I have learnt how the final transition procedure is done in finer detail.

Although it is an incredible achievement, anyone going through gender reassignment from female to male needs to learn and understand that sacrifices need to be made in order to achieve what it is you are searching for. When transitioning, consider at the outset the opportunity to freeze some of your genetic material - eggs or sperm - to enable you to have a better opportunity to parent a child who shares some of your DNA further down the line, but you also lose the ability to climax during sex. Whilst that may seem like a small price to pay, losing the ability to climax takes an edge off the whole love making scenario. But for those going through male to female, you will equally not be able to know the joy of carrying a child as a female would, science is still incapable of transplanting a womb.

Gender reassignment comes with constant daily reminders. If you are trained to spot the signs, you will see a female to male with a scar that spans the whole of their lower forearm. This is where the skin graft comes from to create the new shaft. There can be two downsides which need addressing on a daily basis, one is that by using this area of skin it will grow the natural hair on the shaft, meaning constant shaving. The other is one I have since discovered is also used for males suffering from erectile dysfunction and involves having a pump fitted within the scrotum. This medical intervention is therefore not new.

So, depending on how you view or process things, there are different ways of accepting this. There is one very positive vibe though, you will provide your partner with hours of fun! And that is never a bad thing, if you get my drift.

Male to female also has their price to pay too, with the daily internal workouts which they must perform to make sure their newly formed vagina doesn't close up; not to mention the inclusion of lube to help with the act of love making. Each of these physical interventions is one that others either have no knowledge of or take for granted and misuse.

CHAPTER 22: WHAT I'VE LEARNT ALONG THE WAY ...

From my own experiences, it is clear to see that my mother failed me in every aspect of the parent and child relationship, which paved the way for our volatile untrusting nothingness. Not only did she not protect me from a lifetime of mental and emotional abuse but she also contributed to it, to serve her own purposes. Writing this book has given me the chance to understand and make sense of my own life as a child and what I had had bestowed upon me. It paved the way for doing everything better, to make sure that my children never felt the way I did.

At no point did she ever help me to address my own issues surrounding coping with my brother's transition. Let's be clear though, I have never for one moment ever been against my brother going through gender reassignment. For him, it was by far the best thing for him to do, despite that fact that it aided his bullying and narcissistic ways. What I have struggled with is the lack of support and lack of recognition for the hard times my brother bestowed upon me. He has left me mentally scared, which has been a work in progress every single day for the last thirty five years. Out of everyone involved in along my journey, I am the only one qualified to throw stones but I haven't. I have endeavored to be better than them and not carry on that learnt behaviour.

Having said that and after everything, I am so incredibly grateful to my mother for her teachings, they have been invaluable. She taught me to be a better person than she is and she taught me how to cope with transitioning far better than she did. She grew blinkers and even to this day she still wears them.

I, on the other hand have grown to see and understand the bigger picture, to be the best I can be for my own children and friends that find their way to me. To incorporate everyone's feelings, emotions and needs and not just those of Jack's or my daughter's or my youngest son for that matter. My experience has taught me to remain grounded and open minded as well as acknowledging to myself that I have the right and power to protect myself from people that do me harm both physically, emotionally and mentally. And, that I have no need in ever feeling guilty about doing that.

The long and short of it is, my mother failed to help me to navigate my brother's very complex emotions, which were sustained from a young age right through into my adulthood. She also failed her own son, by making him into the tyrant that he is. She has only ever offered her ultimate and blinkered support directly to her son. Using her capacity and ability to accommodate his sole care, wants and needs. In doing so, she has created a monster. But she has not only failed the two of us but has also failed my own family too. She has dropped them twice, disowned them twice, and played vicious mind games with the most vulnerable of them and never once acknowledged the damage she caused or the role she has played in it. Who in their right mind does that to innocent children, not to mention their own flesh and blood?

She has never once supported them. Instead she has used and abused her eldest grandson by making him hateful and bigoted and by twisting events in his life into untruths. Again, why would anyone do that to a child?

My mother has failed the next generation that Arron may go on to produce, because he will continue this line of learnt behaviour and think it acceptable. My mother is most defiantly no martyr, she has failed more people than she can comprehend.

Unless Arron is willing to change, I pity any grandchildren born to him, because if they are any different to him, then they will learn that he does not have the tools or capability to provide them with a safe space or loving home. This would be a tragedy, this is where learnt behaviour comes from and if we are to change the world, we need to start at home. Home is where you are meant to feel safe, home is where you should be able to be yourself.

As for my brother, it is unfortunate that his hatred and jealousy for me runs far too deep and will clearly remain with him for all eternity. There is nothing more I can do about it or am willing to do about it. The problem doesn't actually lie with me and it has actually taken me 42years to work that out.

Throughout the process of my brother's transition, his mental attitude hasn't changed and that is really sad.

Having come through a huge mental struggle himself, he lacks the understanding and compassion needed to help others or to see anyone else's needs above his own.

Jack, on the other hand, has changed everything about himself. The process has helped him mature into a caring, thoughtful and engaging human being who thinks about a situation from all angles before acting. He incorporates emotion, both mental and physical, which is a rare talent.

Very sadly I won't allow my brother to put me through more or allow him to impose on me anymore. He and I have come as far as we ever will in this lifetime. I wish him well. I don't even wish anything bad for him; I just hope he gets everything he deserves.

I want to go back to my original question: which came first, being a daughter or a sister? From the day I was created I became a daughter and a sister. Yet my mother never saw me as a daughter, least of all hers. She never recognised me as one and never treated me as one. In fact, she did everything within her power to obliterate me.

Likewise, my sister didn't want me to be her sister. She had no need for a sister, nor for anyone else for that matter. As my sister didn't treat me as a sister, I am therefore a sister to no one. I have grown up and become wise to all the little things that have happened and I realise that on that very same day of creation, I was in fact relinquished of my duties as both sister and daughter.

I am now reclassified and redefined first and foremost as a mother. I am a mother to four incredible children who have entrusted their needs into my care and who have had the courage to fulfil their natural born instincts under my guidance. They have had a safe space and place to discover who they are and who they want to be. I am so incredibly proud of them and honoured to accompany them on their individual life journeys. I am also mother to my eldest son, whether he chooses to acknowledge that or not, I can not answer for him. I know that I watch him from afar and track his life good and bad and up's and down's. I wish him every success and I am sad that he doesn't want to be a part of our family. I am sadder to acknowledge that he damages mental health not only for myself but his siblings, I am not sure that I would ever trust him with such a delicate issue ever again.

Along the way, I have also learnt how hard the whole process of transitioning is. Not just for the person needing or requiring transition, but for those other people involved too. It is most definitely not just one person that goes through the process of transgender or any other transition. It is a complex merry go round of emotions which for some is completely uncharted territory and should be handled with care and compassion from all angles and sides. It is a lengthy process that is never ending and at some points throughout the journey, it needs to be revisited and tweaked. I am not sure that anyone untrained truly realises just how complex the mental health side of transitioning is. In layman's term, it should be seen as an onion, it is multilayered and needs to be peeled back slowly and carefully in order not to break it. There needs to be more in place right and a reform from the start of the educational system. We need to support the current generation and all future generations and recognise that gender and sexuality does in fact start from a very early age. We need to see children as their own people and stop putting them into boxes and conditioning them to other ways of thinking. We need to retrain teachers and people in the educational system to leave their thoughts, beliefs and prejudices at the door and teach with an open heart and mind. Otherwise why are they teaching in the first place. Teachers also needs to acknowledge that they too can be damaging and detrimental to students mental health and overall wellbeing. We all need to take stock of how we support children from an early age upwards.

I have also learnt that for whatever reason only beknown to Jack and my brother, they have been very similar in a lot of their approaches and are quite insular in their approach to friends and family in dealing with their transition. They have behaved as if they are an island, but in reality both have needed the company and support of their family, as they have transitioned and subsequently. They have both wanted to slide under the radar and present as they are and while I do understand that fact, the fact remains that there will inevitable times when it does crop up and the awkward conversation will have to be had.

I know from my point of view that I want to talk about it; I need to talk about it and it is totally unfair and unreasonable to expect and request that people close to them should remain silent. I want to be able to support others going through the process who aren't able to have the support they need. I want to be able to put my head above the parapet and challenge an archaic system. Most importantly, I was asked during an educational meeting, who do I turn to for support, to off load too. The answer is no one. I have been conditioned into coping by myself. But having said that, I have the support from my family. We all have our own different ways in coping with anything and everything, which should be respected. Afterall, we have respected you and the way you have wanted to live your life.

As a sister, I wanted and needed my brother to accept what he put me through. I wanted to hear him say he knew he was the cause and that he was sorry for what he had imposed upon me, but I will never hear him say it. I have realised that the issues between us run far deeper than just his need to transition. My very existence in the same breathing space as him, makes his blood boil, he hates me that much. Through his transition process, I have learnt how to support my children in the best way I know how and I have learnt from my mother how not to do it.

The daily challenges faced by people navigating through LGBTQ+ are taken for granted by people going about their everyday business in their world of what normal represents to them. I've learnt that some people need and rely upon a support network outside of their friends and family because they lack the support from the people who are supposed to be their closest allies; that is really hard for me to accept. I don't understand how those family and friends can't be there for them. It could be because their loved ones don't want to be there for them? Or maybe it is because the person going through LGBTQ+ knows they are better supported by others? That they feel they can only truly be their own person around likeminded people?

If they don't want support or to be a part of it, they have to remember that this journey is not just theirs to travel alone, it is a worldwide community qualifying millions of people, all of whom are crying out for support. Unfortunately, this community does not have a voice which is being heard, and it will take many years to get equality. However, it could be argued that the LGBTQ+ community may not be helping themselves, by bringing in more that fifty genders and pronouns in an attempt to becoming accepted in the way that they feel. Some of those gender names could be seen as an attack on other genders, which is a great shame. We must all stand together if any change is to happen. Everyone has to find their own way along their own path but they need support regardless of how that support package looks.

I have seen how truly wicked the human race can be to its fellow man; when all that person wants to do is go about their life quietly and keep to themselves. I have nothing but admiration for anyone coping with the daily and never-ending hamster wheel of self-hate because their physical self doesn't conform to the mental version of themselves.

The pain I have felt watching not just Jack's pain but Emily's too. Knowing I was unable to ease it, to change it, to take it away there and then, as every mother who wants to protect their child wishes to. The secret knowledge of what I saw and never told Jack, never talked about it, just quietly observing him until he was ready to talk about it.

I have painstakingly watched Jack come to terms with the process he faced and the up-hill struggle for acceptance from a backward society. Not to mention the archaic NHS system that doesn't deliver enough or fast enough, which in turn adds to further distress and loss of life.

I have also seen how ancient military institutes are failing anyone who wishes to be a part of them. They have shown themselves to be the most bigoted of all; with their archaic, outdated and out of touch processes. They could and are missing out on some of the most talented personnel that would serve crown and country, which is a great shame. Everybody should be allowed the right to follow a career path that they have chosen, rather than being forced in to something that will just do.

I am proud of how Jack has faced adversity from people he thought he knew, both outside the family and from within. From his own brother, Arron, and from his extended family, who have thrown the most incredible and bigoted attitudes his way, including disowning him. He has faced his adversity with pride.

We are proud of Jack, we are proud of all of our children because they carry their own different and unique traits, some good, some bad. They have had a lot of adversity thrown at them and I would like to think that we have given them the tools to cope with it. Also to help those around them to cope, both now and with a legacy stretching in to future generations.

Referring back to Nelson Mandela's quote at the start of my book, "No one is born hating another person because of the colour of his skin, or his background, or his religion. People must learn to hate, and if they can learn to hate, they can be taught to love, for love comes more naturally to the human heart than its opposite." We learn from acquired experiences from those around us. If people are uneducated, not just in LGBTQ+, then they will be poorly educating the next generation. Who therefore is to blame?

Children don't see colour of skin, race, gender or religion, they see love and kindness, they gravitate towards those traits. If you then instill hate then that emotion replaces that love and kindness. Is that fair for those people to have uneducated views bestowed on them? Who should be to blame for these attitudes, when the people educating them have been ill educated? Do we not have enough to cope with whilst navigating our own paths without adding in hatred too? Aren't people, no matter how young or old, entitled to have freedom of will and to have the ability to say, "No, I don't want to hear your views; I want to create my own?" If you are not prepared to listen to someone else's view when you demand they listen to yours, what kind of a person does that make you?

This world or should I say the people in it, have created a world in which it is no longer sustainable to keep to archaic ideologies. It needs to, and must, start to relearn how to integrate every walk of life. Over the generations and in particular going back to the 19th century, gender roles were introduced and put into place. Why? What purpose did they serve and who did they serve? Men were told what was expected of them and how to act and equally the same was imposed on women.

But what did it really achieve? It divided the human race and gave power to those who would misuse it. Moving on to the 1940s, gender and race were brought in which further added to the divide in the archaic ideologies war. If society had been raised to be gender neutral we wouldn't be faced with any of the gender issues we have now. I think it is time to retrain society to break down the gender barriers for the sake of future generations.

Above all, I have learnt to fight for equality and I have no fear in sticking my neck out to make those around me feel included. For instance, we attended a wedding fair with a same sex couple who we consider to be very dear friends; every stall holder made a bee-line for me. I clearly walked around with a sign over my head saying I was a bride to be. There is clearly still an automatic thought process that a bride is the female. But I wasn't. Our friends were the ones planning their wedding, so I pointed the stall holders in their direction, which threw them off to say the least. They became tongue tied and fidgety, hurrying through their sales pitches. Why? I really don't know; I can't answer that. I would make a point of pulling stall holders up on their display, where they only had, Mr & Mrs signs and displays, "Where's the Mr & Mr?" and, "Oh, it would be lovely to see a 'Mrs & Mrs. It's a shame you don't advertise diversity." I'm not afraid to say my piece now and I'm not afraid of offending anyone else, because these attitudes are offensive to the people I'm with.

I've learnt that this world is full of diversity but how sad it is that people are so stuck in their own ways that they can't see and accept it. Those people are the ones that truly miss out on the beauty of life. They do not understand that life is a gift. Yet another example is sadly applied to my children's other grandparents, my first husband's parents.

Unbeknown to me, Jack had made contact with them after our move back to the coast. He was particularly excited about seeing his cousins and getting reacquainted with them and had arranged to meet up with his paternal grandparents as well as his cousins on the same night. Jack hadn't told his grandparents about his journey and had presented himself as Jack and not their granddaughter. I can understand why he didn't and I can understand why my ex in-laws reacted the way they did. Not even his own father wants anything to do with him since learning of his transition.

If Jack had come to me and told me of his plans, I would have told him how they had reacted to the news when my brother was starting the same journey. It may have saved him the hurt and disappointment of rejection.

But this is how we grow strong and know for certain that we have the right people surrounding us at the right time. It's incredibly sad to think that this thought process has led to a knock-on effect with the cousins who are the same generation as my children. How are we to ever rid learnt behaviour from society and to teach everyone that they have the right to free will and freedom of their own thoughts, beliefs and identities without fear of persecution and rejection?

My partner is proof that we can change learnt behaviour. He openly admits that he had no concept of anything to do with LGBTQ+ and would shy away from what made him uncomfortable. This partly has to do with learnt behaviour from his upbringing but also because he was never educated on anything other than being a heterosexual.

Having been very much a part of Jack's process and that of Emily's, he has learnt to overcome his learnt behaviour and accept that there is a real need to change how LGBTQ+ is viewed and accepted. He has learnt to understand in finer detail the mental aspect that others go through and he has learnt how best to support my children and our close friends. I am very grateful that he has allowed himself to be openminded enough to change and to be a part of all of our journeys.

My final thought goes to those in power who are desperately seeking change but constantly come up against those who don't want it. Let's take the Scottish Parliament as an example of this, they are seeking to reform the Gender Bill, they want progress, they want change, they are wishing to move forward and recognise the need in doing so. However, the British Government are thwarting this progress at every turn. Why? What purpose does this serve for the British Government? Why can't they accept that we need to change? Why aren't they allowing every human the same right of existence? The German Government is the same.

We need to start calling out all these global governments and highlighting them for what they are. Surely with the added delay in medical treatment, which affects so many lives, they should be held accountable. Why aren't LGBTQ+ people given the same rights as heterosexual people? Please explain to me what the difference is, because I am failing to understand it. These delays bring heartache and misery to so many. Why aren't the British Government prepared to relinquish this gender power over our nation?

I am also saddened at having reached out to so many people who have gone through gender reassignment to ask for their support with this book but they haven't wanted to share it. I have also reached out to private and NHS gender reassignment clinics to ask for their support and sponsorship, but they too have failed to recognise the importance of what this book aims to achieve. These rejections are incredibly sad and a further blow in the fight for LGBTQ+ equalities and acceptance. It further highlights that as far as they are concerned LGBQT+ is just money driven, otherwise they would see and understand the importance of supporting the mental aspects too.

We need more movements like the “Me Too”, “She said” and “Free the Nipple Movement”.

We need more people making a stand. One person can’t shout loud enough to be heard, but two people can shout louder, three people can shout loudest and hundreds of people can be heard shouting from the rooftops of buildings.

EPILOGUE

At the beginning of the Prologue, I asked you to consider and write down your version of normal. Now having finished the story, has your version of normal changed? Has it challenged what you have grown up thinking normal was and is? Has it redefined normal to you? Has it opened your mind to a new ever evolving normal, which needs to move with the times?

Has it highlighted that the LGBTQ+ community lacks the same human rights power or movement as the heterosexual community? And has it shown what level of power governments all over the world have in keeping the LGBTQ+ community hidden out of sight, squashing their efforts as a civilised society which strives to achieve progress?

Going back to the definitions of what civilisation means, I have come across the following:

"The stage of human social and cultural development and organisation that is considered most advanced."

"The process of educating a society so that its culture becomes more developed."

"Human society with its well-developed social and organisations, or the culture and way of life of a society or country at a particular period in time."

And a definition of Progress:

"Forward or onward movement towards a destination or develop towards an improved or more advanced condition."

For one reason or another, ninety per cent of the world population are unhappy in the form they currently occupy. I would say that eighty-nine per cent of those people never make the necessary changes which would enable them to lead a happier life.

Is it that their own mental or physical wellbeing doesn't mean enough to them to want to change anything?

Or quite simply they don't have what it takes to make those changes?

Could it be that the society they have been brought up in is more vitriolic to change and that they are afraid to break the barriers?

This is where most damage is done. It's other people's imposed beliefs that hinder someone else from following their true path. It's the fear of breaking the norm and being disrespectful towards someone else that stops anyone in their tracks. What they don't realise is that the one person they are most being disrespectful towards is themselves.

However, for those people who do actually make these huge leaps of faith, they should be so incredibly proud of themselves.

It takes belief. Belief in yourself that you are worth the long hard road that you might have to travel.

Faith in yourself and in the people that you have surrounded and entrusted your journey to. Those people who will love, encourage and support you.

Finally, courage, courage to make the necessary changes. Courage to face adversity head on and stand your ground for what you believe in. Courage to change your life so that you can be in that one per cent happiness club.

Not everyone can manage to pull this off, not everyone has the courage to break that norm and seek what they truly want and need.

My advice to anyone is this, whatever your child identifies as, whatever your sibling identifies as and whatever your friend identifies as, respect them for it, love them for it and cherish them for it. They have courage in themselves that is beyond comparison to your own. It takes a massive amount of all the above to chase your dreams, to find that one per cent of happiness and to grasp it.

My partner was ill-educated in issues surrounding sexuality and gender and how that ill-education has done him wrong in the years prior, along with others he has met along his journey in life. He constantly says to me that every day is a learning day. No matter how small the topic is or how useless the knowledge is, you have to want to be open enough to learn, and to want to learn, in order to change your thought processes. We talk about issues all the time; we never stop talking about them and he thanks us all for our openness about everything and feels it has helped him greatly. We all need to start talking about subjects we find difficult, sex, birth, death, love, emotions etc. They all have a place in the world and in all of our lives, therefore we need to embrace them.

And I ask you, do you have what it takes to grab your dreams, to live your best life and to find your one per cent of happiness? Because if you don't, you don't have the right to not show respect to those who do. Regardless of who or what they identify as. You don't have the right to put your two pennies worth in and you don't have the right to judge their worth over your own. People need to address their own insecurities and lack of self-worth, vision and compassion towards a fellow human being before they are able to bring their voice to the table.

For those of you who are parents and haven't been able to accept transitioning or LGBTQ+ in any form: not only have you failed as a human being, but you have also failed as a parent. It is not your job or right to pass judgement on your children, on what or who they need to be. It is your job to nurture, love, protect and guide them into becoming the best possible version of themselves. That means in whatever form that child takes.

Don't be selfish.

This isn't about you.

It's about them.

Your child and fellow human.

Please also remember that none of us who are living

and breathing here today ever asked to be here. We didn't have our say before being conceived; we weren't given a choice, so we must accept whatever form we are here in. As well as accepting all other people's forms.

If you are capable of giving your child your last breath in order to save them, then you are capable of accepting them in any form. It takes two people to make another human being, so let's not forget that this journey is not yours alone. It is theirs too. They have a right to be happy in whatever form that takes, just as you have sought happiness in the form you have taken. You need to hold them, love them, cherish them but most of all to respect them for who they are.

Following a pursuit of happiness is no easy job for anyone and most of us don't even follow it; we settle for the easy option. Whatever label anyone has, remember they have just as much right to wear that label as anyone else. Whether it's transgender, LGBTQ+, nonbinary, heterosexual, the list is endless, these labels should be our new normal.

For all those people out there who are not LGBTQ+ or any of the never-ending list of labels that follow, you are going against the norm and I have this to say, it is you that is now outnumbered and going against the norm. There are more people going against your version of normal nowadays than ever before.

So, back to the definition I quoted at the start of my book, "Something that is normal is usual and ordinary. Normal can also be used to describe individual behaviour that conforms to the most common behaviour. Therefore, normal must be classed as more than one."

Hold on to that thought because for everyone following their chosen LGBTQ+ path, YOU are normal, YOU are valued, and YOU are loved AS YOU ARE. It may not be by the people you would like it to be by, but you are loved, nevertheless.

I have come across and had the absolute pleasure of meeting the most amazing LGBTQ+ people. They carry with them so much pride, colour, love, care and compassion, it puts others to utter shame.

Despite the fact that when I look in the mirror, I may not have been happy with this lump or that bump, I have always been happy with myself as a person and content with what and who I am. Don't get me wrong, the thought of being a man has appealed at certain points throughout my life because of what society has defined as a weakness for being female, but I have learnt to be happy with who I am.

No one can imagine what it feels like to not be happy, can you? Can you imagine what it must feel like realising one day that you don't quite fit into the body you have and that something feels wrong about it? Knowing there is no receipt to take it back and change it. Knowing that in order to live your life you have to bind yourself to within an inch of your life. Or to stuff a bralette to make it appear you have breasts. That you do these things regardless of how much physical pain you inflict on yourself. Knowing it's your time of the month and there is nothing you can do about it. That even the medical treatments that have been created and designed to stop it have failed you, because Mother Nature thinks she knows you and your body better than you. That she will win and there's nothing you can do about it.

Could you knowingly look in that mirror and really love the person staring back at you when all you are doing is fighting against it? Your body seems to hate you, whilst your mind screams for release.

Each and every country and government, other than those already seeking to improve their own civilisation and progress, thwarts this progress, they are not willing to allow all humans their human rights. Governments are lacking in understanding and embracing the moral worth of any individual by failing to understand the political and social philosophy that brings about individualism. Surely this could be tantamount to a lawsuit? Could this be challenged at the highest level if enough people started seeing and realising this?

What if you as a heterosexual started having your human rights changed, what would you do to voice it, what level would you go to, to have a say, "Hold on, this isn't right, I have a right too!" To make a difference in anyone's life, you don't have to be brilliant, rich, beautiful or even perfect. You just have to care enough to want to make a difference. I care about the mental wellbeing of anyone that falls under the LGBTQ+ umbrella. That's not to say that I don't care about anyone else, we all have mental wellbeing that needs addressing, but there is more help out there for anyone none LGBTQ+ than there is LGBTQ+. Which is very sad.

What will you do to ensure all humans have equality in their everyday lives?

Printed in Great Britain
by Amazon

24401342R00119